ACCLAIM FOR COLLEEN COBLE

"Coble's atmospheric and suspenseful series launch should appeal to fans of Tracie Peterson and other authors of Christian romantic suspense."

—*LIBRARY JOURNAL*
REVIEW OF *TIDEWATER INN*

"Romantically tense, but with just the right touch of danger, this cowboy love story is surprisingly clever—and pleasingly sweet."

—USAToday.com REVIEW
OF *BLUE MOON PROMISE*

"Colleen Coble will keep you glued to each page as she shows you the beauty of God's most primitive land and the dangers it hides."

—WWW.ROMANCEJUNKIES.COM

"[An] outstanding, completely engaging tale that will have you on the edge of your seat . . . A must-have for all fans of romantic suspense!"

—THEROMANCEREADERSCONNECTION.COM
REVIEW OF *ANATHEMA*

"Colleen Coble lays an intricate trail in *Without a Trace* and draws the reader on like a hound with a scent."

—*ROMANTIC TIMES*, 4½ STARS

"Coble's historical series just keeps getting better with each entry."

—LIBRARY JOURNAL
STARRED REVIEW OF
THE LIGHTKEEPER'S BALL

"Don't ever mistake [Coble's] for the fluffy romances with a little bit of suspense. She writes solid suspense, and she ties it all together beautifully with a wonderful message."

—LIFEINREVIEWBLOG.COM
REVIEW OF LONESTAR ANGEL

"This book has everything I enjoy: mystery, romance, and suspense. The characters are likable, understandable, and I can relate to them."

—THEFRIENDLYBOOKNOOK.COM

"[M]ystery, danger, and intrigue as well as romance, love, and subtle inspiration. *The Lightkeeper's Daughter* is a 'keeper.'"

—ONCEUPONAROMANCE.NET

"Colleen is a master storyteller."

—KAREN KINGSBURY,
BESTSELLING AUTHOR
OF *UNLOCKED* AND
LEARNING

JOURNEY OF THE
HEART COLLECTION

A
HEART'S
Disguise

A
HEART'S
Obsession

A
HEART'S
Danger

ALSO BY COLLEEN COBLE

A

HEART'S

DISGUISE

A

HEART'S

OBSESSION

A

HEART'S

DANGER

THREE NOVELLAS IN ONE

COLLEEN
COBLE

THOMAS NELSON
Since 1798

NASHVILLE   MEXICO CITY   RIO DE JANEIRO

Published in Nashville, Tennessee, by Thomas Nelson. Thomas Nelson is a registered trademark of HarperCollins Christian Publishing, Inc.

Thomas Nelson titles may be purchased in bulk for educational, business, fund-raising, or sales promotional use. For information, please e-mail SpecialMarkets@ThomasNelson.com.

Publisher's Note: This novel is a work of fiction. Names, characters, places, and incidents are either products of the author's imagination or used fictitiously. All characters are fictional, and any similarity to people living or dead is purely coincidental.

ISBN 978-0-7180-3976-9

Printed in the United States of America
15 16 17 18 19 20 RRD 6 5 4 3 2 1

In memory of my brother Randy Rhoads, who taught me to love the mountains of Wyoming, and my grandparents Everett and Eileen Everroad, who loved me unconditionally. May you walk those heavenly mountains with joy.

TABLE OF CONTENTS

A
HEART'S
DISGUISE

ONE

WABASH, INDIANA, OCTOBER 1865

Autumn's chill matched Sarah Montgomery's heart. The war had taken so much from her, and it seemed impossible for life to ever get to a hopeful place. The scent of turning leaves lingered in the air as she sat on a porch rocking chair beside her father, who was huddled in a blanket. Her bustle bunched under her uncomfortably, but she wanted to be close to her ill father for as long as possible before Ben arrived.

The sun lingered on the horizon, casting rays of gold and red across the Indiana sky. In the distance, she could see the silhouettes of the workers in the field as they tossed the last of the ears of corn into the wagon behind the horses.

"Bed sounds better than a party." She stifled a yawn. "I'm getting tired of dances every night, though I can't begrudge everyone's revelry." The Union was preserved, but the price had been so high. Scarcely a family in the county had been spared the loss of a loved one.

Her father coughed and tugged the blanket higher on his chest. "I'm glad you're beginning to enjoy life again. Rand wouldn't want you to grieve."

"No. No, he wouldn't." But what no one seemed to understand was that her fiancé's death in the war had left a hole that couldn't be filled. Not ever.

His cold hand clamped down on her wrist. "I need to see you settled before I die, Sarah."

She flinched. "Don't talk like that, Papa." She couldn't bear to lose him—not when she'd already lost so much.

He rubbed his forehead. "You heard the doctor as plainly as I did last week. This old ticker isn't going to hold out much longer. I want you to marry Ben Croftner. He'll be a good husband to you."

Sarah wanted to bolt from the porch, to hide herself in the dusty golden stalks and forget her father's request. "Ben isn't Rand. I don't think I can do it."

"Rand is never coming back, honey. Do you want to live here in this house with Wade the rest of your life?"

She looked down at the bowl of corn in her hands. "No."

Her older brother thought he always knew best, and the two of them had never gotten along. "What about Joel?" She'd raised her eight-year-old brother from infancy when their mother died in childbirth. Any future she might plan had to include Joel.

"He should go with you. Wade is too hard on him, and he wouldn't do well without you." Her father coughed away a wheeze.

She couldn't believe she was actually thinking about it, but what other choice did she have? She liked Ben well enough. He had a nice home along the Wabash River, and he was always kind to Joel.

"I'll think about it," she said as Ben's carriage came into view.

Ben swung Sarah around the dance floor past hay bales, bridles, and plows. The fiddle and the melody lifted her spirits, dampened by so much death and heartache. Women in hoop skirts and men in top hats had thrown off the heartache of the War Between the States tonight as they dipped and swayed on the barn floor. The food shortages had eased some, and the aroma of apple pie—a scarcity with the lack of sugar—wafted through the space.

Ben was such a fine dancer, strong and graceful in a way that made her feel she could float across the floor in his arms. He grinned down at her, sensing perhaps that she was beginning to enjoy herself just a little, for once.

Ben tightened his grip around her waist possessively. "Come outside a minute, would you, Sarah? I want to talk to you." His smile was warm, but his firm voice brooked no objection. She let him lead her toward the big sliding door of the barn, beyond wooden tables piled high with pumpkin rolls and pies of every imaginable flavor, past the seated older women who watched their exit with wistful smiles.

As Ben led her into the cool of the evening, Sarah's weariness gave way to a rising dread. After her father's request before the dance, she suspected Ben had already mentioned his intentions to her family. She wasn't ready.

Her steps faltered as she hung back. "Wait, Ben. Let me get my shawl." Her hands shaking, she took her blue shawl from a peg on the wall and wrapped it around her shoulders.

"Come on, Sarah." His face purposeful and his voice impatient, Ben tugged on her arm and drew her outside.

The full moon shone down on them, but the most light came from the lanterns strung around the graying barn and through the muddy yard. The lights dipped and swayed like fireflies in the light breeze. The air was moist and tangy, a mixture of ripening grain and the smoke from a bonfire in the adjoining field. The October night had a slight chill, and Sarah pulled her shawl more closely about her shoulders.

Ben pulled Sarah down onto a bench away from several other couples watching the bonfire shoot sparks high into the darkening sky. "It's time we talked about our future, Sarah." He hesitated as if gauging her reaction. "I want to marry you. You know how I've felt about you for years, and now that Rand's gone—well, I hope you'll consider me."

Sarah raised a trembling hand to her throat and felt her pulse fluttering under her fingertips. How did she tell him Rand still occupied her heart? That she would never love anyone again? She swallowed hard, but the words stuck in her throat.

Did she have the obligation to make others happy when it was in her power? She owed it to Papa to get her life settled. How could she refuse to do whatever it took to ease her father's worries? And besides, what else did the future hold except to be someone's wife? Like her father had said, she didn't want to live with Wade the rest of her life.

She stared up into Ben's earnest face. "What about Joel? I can't go anywhere without him."

"I know that, honey. He's more like your own boy than your brother. We have plenty of bedrooms. I hope to fill the rest of them with babies Joel can be a big brother to."

His words eased the ache in her heart somewhat. Didn't Joel deserve a more normal life too? Ben was a good man, a successful man. He'd make sure she and

Joel never wanted for anything. What more could she really hope for? "All right. I'll marry you."

Ben smiled in spite of her lackluster response. "I'm so glad, my dear. You won't be sorry."

Her stomach sank as she twisted her icy hands in the folds of her skirt. *I already am.*

"Shall we go announce our good news?" Without waiting for her answer, he drew her up and tucked her hand into the crook of his elbow. "Your family will be so pleased."

She pushed her shoulders back and held her head erect as they walked into the barn. She could do this, for her family. For her father and brothers.

Ben pulled her with him to the front of the room and waved his hands. "Ladies and gentlemen, may I have your attention?"

The music stopped with a last, dying squeal of the fiddle, and flushed couples stared back at them. Her cheeks burned and Sarah took a deep, calming breath. She caught her dear friend Amelia's stricken look and nodded encouragingly.

Sarah glanced up at Ben. He was so good-looking, though in a different way than Rand had been. Ben's hair was blond, almost white, and he had gray eyes the color of the Wabash River on a stormy day. He had a self-confident air, and his charm smoothed most obstacles he encountered. Like her father had said, she would never want for anything as Ben's wife. *Except for love.*

Ben dropped a possessive arm around her shoulders. "You all know how long I've tried to get Sarah to agree to be my wife."

"I always thought she showed a lot of sense," called Jason Maxwell from up in the haymow, where a group of young men had been playing checkers. Some adolescent boys who'd been watching the game hooted with laughter. "The prettiest girl in town ought to be able to do better than you."

Ben laughed, too, but there was little humor in his eyes. "Well, you can all congratulate me—she finally gave in! You're all invited to the wedding—and it'll be a humdinger!"

Friends and neighbors crowded around quickly to congratulate them, and Sarah was hugged and kissed as she fought to keep her smile from slipping. Wade grinned smugly as he shook Ben's hand.

Joel came over for a quick embrace. "What about me?"

She was the only one who heard his whisper, and

she pulled him close. "Ben says you can live with us. It will be like a real home, honey. You'll see. And you can go see Papa anytime you like. We'll live close."

His smile came then, and he released his tight grip on her. Over his shoulder, she saw the two Campbell boys, Rand's brothers, making their way away from the party. What must they think of her? When Joel turned to speak to Ben, she ducked away quietly and hurried to intercept them.

They stopped beside the heavily laden tables to wait for her. Before she could say a word, Jacob took her hand in his, his dark eyes, so like his older brother's, sad in spite of his smile. "No need to worry about us, Sarah. We saw this coming. Besides, Rand wouldn't want you to grieve forever. We just want you to be happy. Right, Shane?"

The youngest Campbell pushed his blond hair out of his face and turned sober blue eyes on her. "Right. The only thing is—" He hesitated and looked from Jacob to Sarah. "What if Rand's not really dead?"

Sarah gasped. "What on earth do you mean?" There was a faint flutter of hope in her chest. Did they know something they hadn't told her? Shane held his tongue. "What does he mean, Jacob?" she asked.

"Rand is dead. Ben saw his body in Andersonville. Father got official notification from the army. And his name was on the list in the newspaper."

"But we never got his body or his things." Shane's chin jutted out. "There could still be some mistake. Maybe he was wounded real bad. Maybe Ben was wrong."

Jacob frowned at his brother. "Shane, that's enough. It's been over a year since he was reported dead. Don't you think Rand would have written? Or the army would have contacted us? It's no wonder we didn't get his body back or his things. The casualties were too overwhelming. Thousands were buried in unmarked graves. Both Union and Rebs. I know— I was there at the Battle of Chickamauga. We don't know how he died, but I have no doubt he's gone. You have to face the truth, Shane."

Shane's eyes shone with unshed tears, and Sarah fought tears of her own. She didn't think she would ever get used to the reality of Rand's death, but she understood why Jacob was being so brutal. Shane couldn't begin to heal until he accepted it. Just as she was finally beginning to accept it.

Jacob put a comforting arm around Shane's

shoulders as tears trickled down the youngster's cheeks. "I'm sorry, Sarah. I had no idea such a notion was brewing in that brain of his. Forget what he said and just be happy." He reached out and touched her cheek. "Ben's a lucky guy. But remember, whatever happens, you'll always be a part of our family too."

"Thank you, Jacob. I'll remember," she whispered as she watched them thread their way through the throng.

There was a soft touch on her arm, and she whirled, thinking it was Ben, that he would see her tears. But it was just Amelia, her blue eyes anxious. "You're crying. Are you all right?"

"Oh yes. It's just those Campbell boys. They're so sweet . . ."

Amelia laughed. "I am awfully fond of Jacob."

"Good thing you're marrying him then, isn't it?" The two friends laughed and hugged. Amelia held Sarah at arm's length and leveled her gaze. "Are you being honest with me? You're not crying about Ben's announcement?"

"No, of course not," Sarah objected, a little more strenuously than she meant to. "I'm thrilled!"

"Now I know you're lying to me."

"I know you don't approve of Ben, but this is really for the best. Wade says . . ."

"Wade says? When did Wade ever say a sensible thing in his life? Just tell me this: Can you look me in the eyes and tell me you love Ben?"

Sarah pressed her lips together. Amelia always cut right through to the heart of the matter. "Amelia, I know you mean well, but that question gets us nowhere. I have to marry soon or I'll die a spinster in Wade's home." She shuddered. "And Ben loves me." The excuses sounded weak, even to her own ears. "It may not be the life I'd dreamed of or hoped for, but Ben can provide a good life for me."

Amelia hesitated, eyeing Sarah. "You know I want that for you. You deserve that and more. But why Ben? I don't think you love him."

"I like him well enough. Since he got back from the war, he's about the most popular man to walk the streets of Wabash." Sarah nodded toward the cluster of young ladies hovering around Ben in the middle of the floor. "I know a couple of girls who would give anything to be in my shoes. Be happy for me, Amelia. Please? Will you stand up for me and be my bridesmaid?"

Amelia sighed. "Of course I will, if we're still here. Jacob's leave is almost over. He has to report for duty at Fort Laramie soon. When is the wedding?"

"We haven't set a date yet, but don't worry—you'll still be the first bride." Sarah didn't know how she could stand to be separated from her best friend. From across the barn, Ben motioned for her to join him. "I've got to go, but we'll get together tomorrow and make some plans. Okay?" She hurried off, pinning her smile back on.

By the time all the well-wishing and hugging were over, the rest of Sarah's family had left to go home. She'd hoped they'd all be in bed by the time Ben dropped her off.

At Sarah's house, a dim light still shone through the parlor window's lace curtains as Ben helped her down from the buggy. The window was open, and she could smell the aroma of fresh-brewed coffee. Evidently no one was going to bed anytime soon.

He leaned down to kiss her. "You've made me very happy tonight, my dear."

She flinched a bit as his lips grazed her cheek. She'd better get used to it. Ben grasped her waist and started to pull her closer. In spite of her resolve, Sarah quickly pulled away from his grip. "I'd better go in. My father is waiting up. I'll see you tomorrow?"

She rushed up the stairs without waiting for a reply, her heart lightening a bit with every step. When she walked onto the wide front porch, she glanced back. Ben watched her with an unsmiling stare. Had she upset him?

She dragged her eyes from his gaze and called out a cheerful "Good night," hoping she'd misread his look. Weary from the long night, she pushed herself through the front door.

The murmur of voices echoed from the parlor. She hung her shawl on a hook and walked into the room. The thick rug muffled her footsteps, but Wade looked up from the overstuffed chintz chair beside the fireplace. Her father lay on the matching sofa, his breathing labored and his face pale in the dying light from the fireplace.

She quickly knelt at his side. "Papa, are you all right? Should I call Doc Seth?"

"No, no. I'm fine. Just tired." His breathing seemed

to ease as he took her hand and drew her into an embrace. "You remind me so much of your mama the first time I met her." He closed his eyes and grimaced. "I'm going to miss you when you go. It will be almost like losing her again."

Wade's wife came into the parlor carrying a tray laden with cups of steaming coffee. Sarah reached for her sister-in-law's burden. "Here, Rachel. Let me take that. It's much too heavy for you in your condition." Sarah eyed the gentle bulge under Rachel's skirt.

Rachel handed it over with a tired smile of thanks and a glance at her husband.

Wade took a cup of coffee. "Congratulations, Sarah. Ben is quite a catch. Just see you don't forget your family when you're rich."

Was money all he ever thought about? Sarah bit back an angry retort. She didn't want to upset her father. "Why would you say such a thing? You know money isn't important to me."

Wade laughed. "It's all right. You'll see soon enough the difference money makes in this world. Besides, I always thought you could do better than Campbell."

Sarah curled her fingers into her palms and inhaled

to fire back a comment. Wade would never listen to her anyway.

Her father's tender gaze lingered on her. "You were only eleven when your mama died, much too young to take over the household and your new brother the way you did." He wiped a shaking hand across his brow, beaded with drops of sweat. "But I just was so blinded by my own grief, I wasn't thinking clearly. All these years you've managed our home like it was your own. It's time for you to leave here and have your own life, your own home."

Wade slammed his coffee cup down on the table, and some of it sloshed onto the polished walnut surface. "Sure, Sarah played house, but I was always out in the fields working my fingers to the bone to support this family. If not for my hard work, this place would have gone on the auction block long ago. You never seem to remember we all worked together."

His father looked up at him. "You're right, son. I don't tell you often enough how grateful I am that you shouldered the responsibility." He sat up and swung his legs off the couch. "You get on up to bed now. That's where I'm headed."

At least his voice seemed stronger.

Her father laid a gentle hand on her arm. "Why don't you go on up to bed? You can tell us all about your plans tomorrow."

Her anger faded, and she gave a weary nod. It didn't do any good to argue with Wade anyway. He had never liked Rand, probably because he was one of the few people Wade couldn't intimidate. She kissed her father and bid them all good night, then walked upstairs, running her hand along the smooth oak banister. She looked back down into the entryway as she thought about her father's words. She was going to miss this place.

Once in the sanctuary of her room, she stepped out of her hoopskirt and crinoline and struggled with the buttons on her dress. She looked around her bedroom. She'd miss this house, this large room furnished with dainty white furniture stenciled with pink. A lacy coverlet topped the feather bed, and dozens of pastel pillows offered a plump, safe haven to curl up and read. Rand had made the bed for their wedding before he went off to war, and it wouldn't be appropriate to take it with her to Ben's. The very thought was hideous.

She took the pins from her long hair and let it fall

to her shoulders, then pulled her nightgown over her head. She smoothed the two braids loose, then ran her brush through the tresses before rebraiding it in one long plait.

The smooth sheets welcomed her, and she pulled her feather comforter up to her chin. She was filled with a strange foreboding as Shane's words came back to her. *"What if Rand's not really dead?"* She'd indulged in such daydreams in the first months after his death. But tonight the idea followed her into her dreams.

TWO

After a long day of negotiating with the railroad for some land he owned, Ben approached the stately brick two-story with a profound sense of pride. Everything he wanted was within his grasp. He swung off his fine quarter horse and led him into the barn, calling for the stable boy.

Who would have thought that Ben Croftner, son of the good-for-nothing drifter Max Croftner, would pull himself up by his own bootstraps out of the dirt and live in a house that was the envy of everyone in

Wabash—and Indiana, for that matter? He'd done what he had to do to get to the top. There had been much opportunity since the war, and he discovered he had an aptitude for exploiting it. He'd made a fortune the last six months.

And now Sarah Montgomery was finally his. Beautiful Sarah with her mesmerizing green eyes and red-gold hair. He'd be the envy of the men in town, few though they were.

He wiped his dusty shoes on the rug by the door, then stepped into the elegantly appointed front parlor. Velvet drapes, fine walnut tables and Dresden figurines, a plush rug imported from France, and an overstuffed horsehair sofa and chair. He frowned as he saw the figure on the sofa. Too bad he couldn't just leave his family behind the same way he'd left his old life.

Labe jumped up from the sofa, clutching an envelope. "I'm not going to do it anymore, Ben." His voice quivered as he handed over the envelope. "My boss at the post office almost caught me this time. And I'm not going to jail for nobody. Not even you."

Ben patted Labe's shoulder. "Don't worry, little brother. Sarah finally gave in last night. By the time the next letter comes, she'll be my wife."

Labe's mouth dropped open. "Congratulations, then. I never thought you'd really pull it off. When you came back from the war with this crazy scheme, I thought fighting them Rebs had made you loco."

Ben laughed as he sank into the plushness of the high-backed chair and took off his sweat-stained Stetson and wiped his face. Labe wasn't the first to underestimate his ambition. "Like I said, it's all over. Now all you have to do is keep your mouth shut."

He looked at the envelope in his lap. "I suppose I should read what this says." Ben ripped open the top and took out the single sheet of paper. "Won't Mr. High and Mighty Rand Campbell be surprised when he finds his beloved Sarah is married to me!"

He settled more comfortably in his chair and scanned the sprawling lines. His smile faded and a scowl twisted his face. He ripped the page to shreds, tossed them onto the fire burning in the grate, and stood.

"What is it, Ben?"

"Rand's coming home. But no matter. He'll be too late." He strode out the door without another word to Labe.

He flung the harness over his horse's still-damp

neck and hitched up the buggy. As he flicked the buggy whip over the horse's head and headed toward the Montgomery farm, he pressed his lips together with determination. He hadn't kept up a charade for five months to lose Sarah now.

He'd been so careful, so patient, telling her how he'd found Rand in the prison camp and got him to the hospital, only for him to die there. And Rand *should* have died. He'd been just a shell of a man with his skin stretched over his bones when he was finally liberated from Andersonville. It was the most hideous thing Ben had ever seen. But he had rallied, much to Ben's dismay. He really hadn't expected Rand to recuperate as fast as he had, and now he threatened to spoil all Ben's carefully laid plans. Ben couldn't let that happen. He wouldn't.

Sarah was sweeping the front porch when Ben stepped down out of the buggy. She forced herself to relax and lift a hand in greeting when he approached. How good-looking he was. His blond hair just curled over his collar, and his gray eyes were gentle and tender, dispelling her misgivings from the night before. She was doing the right thing.

Ben bounded up the steps with a smile and took her hand. "How's my lovely lady today?"

She smiled up at him. "I'm getting behind in my housework. Everyone has been stopping by to congratulate me. News travels fast."

"Especially good news." He guided her down onto the porch steps and sat beside her. "I was talking to Labe, and he was saying how good it would be to have a real woman doing for us once you and I are married. We haven't decided on a date yet, but I was hoping to make it on my birthday next weekend. Could you be ready?"

"But, Ben, that's only eight days." Panic rose in her throat, and she tried to keep the dismay out of her face as she stared at him. "There's such a lot to do."

"You can be ready, I'm sure, if you really want to be." A note of impatience crept into his voice. "Don't you think you've made me wait long enough?"

"But I have to make my dress. And—"

"I surely don't care what you wear. Your Sunday dress will do just fine."

She lowered her eyes. Why did he always make

her feel so guilty, so indebted to him? "I can be ready. Would you like some iced tea?"

"No, I have a meeting in town. I'll see you tonight."

She allowed his hug, then, with something that felt like relief, watched him ride away. What difference did it really make anyway? One date was as good as another if she was really going to go through with it. And besides, if she wanted Amelia to be her bridesmaid, they'd have to wed before Amelia and Jacob left for Fort Laramie.

Dinner was yet to be made, but Sarah untied her apron and started toward the McCallister farm. She needed to see her friend. She paused at the knoll overlooking Amelia's home. The hills were green with giant oak and maple trees. Several milk cows grazed on the thick, lush grass under a bowl of blue sky. Doctor Seth and his family still lived in the log home he'd built when he first arrived twenty years ago. With his thriving practice, he could well afford an elaborate home in town. But she was glad the McCallisters had never moved. It was her second home, and she ran over the meadow that separated the two properties.

The house had been added on to over the years and now sprawled carelessly in several directions. Their two families had been close ever since Sarah could remember. At one time there was hope that Amelia would marry Wade, but she lost interest as Wade grew to manhood and became the arrogant, self-righteous boor he was. Now Amelia had eyes for no other man but Jacob Campbell.

Amelia was on the wide front porch, churning butter. She greeted Sarah with a smile, her face flushed with exertion. "I was just coming to see you as soon as I was finished." Tendrils of dark hair clung in curls around her face. "I have some ideas for the wedding." Her welcoming smile faded. "What's wrong?"

"I don't know what to do." Sarah launched into an explanation of Ben's plans.

Amelia started shaking her head before Sarah finished. "Eight days! That isn't enough time to get everything ready."

"I know! I tried to tell him that, but he wouldn't listen. He wants to be married on his birthday." Sarah slumped down onto a step. "And I guess it's the least I can do after all I've put him through these past five months. You know how patient he's been . . ." Her voice faltered when she saw the skeptical look Amelia threw her way, and Sarah realized how ridiculous she sounded. "Besides, if we wait until after your wedding, you might have to leave before mine."

"I suppose you're right," Amelia said slowly. "But I've never understood why you think you owe Ben anything. He hasn't done anything special for you." She came to sit next to Sarah on the step. "You say Ben loves you. I'm sure that's true. Who wouldn't? But do you really know his heart, Sarah? Does he know you don't love him?"

"Don't start, Amelia. Please."

Amelia recoiled at her uncharacteristic harshness.

"I'm sorry." Sarah hugged her friend. "It's just that I have to go through with it. Papa wants to see me settled before . . ." She bit her lip. "And besides"— she gave Amelia a wink—"I was thinking how nice it will be to get away from Wade and his constant disapproval."

Amelia smiled and blinked away her tears. "He just needs the Lord in his life."

Sarah was a little envious of her friend's faith. No matter what happened, Amelia seemed to trust God. She never had a bad word to say about anyone.

That's why her attitude toward Ben was so perplexing. But really, this was for the best if Amelia could just see it. Sarah would make a fresh start with Ben, and as the years passed and she had children to occupy her time, maybe the pain in her heart would ease.

The next few days sped by as Sarah threw herself into wedding preparations. Papa had bought her a Singer treadle sewing machine. Her dress, even with its yards and yards of soft, creamy lace, quickly took shape under its whirring needle. She fell into bed each night too exhausted to think or even to dream.

Friday afternoon she sat back and massaged her aching neck thankfully. It was finally finished. She stared out the living room window at the weeping willows swaying along the riverbank. The soft breeze, laden with the rich scent of the Wabash River, blew through the sheer curtains and caressed her hot face.

A memory of walking hand in hand with Rand along the river's edge hit her, and she clutched her skirt, anguish burning in her belly. Why couldn't she stop thinking about him? She'd be Mrs. Ben Croftner in a few days. Then maybe all the ghosts would be laid to rest.

She jumped as the knocker on the front door clattered. When she opened the door, Pastor Aaron Stevens stood on the porch, turning his hat in his hands. "Pastor. We didn't expect you. I believe Wade and Rachel have gone out for a bit and Father is resting. But won't you come in?"

He followed her into the parlor. "I was out calling on the new family by the river, the Longs, and just thought I'd stop in and see how you're doing."

She pointed to the heap of cream material on the sewing machine. "I just finished my dress."

"Are you all right, Sarah? You look . . ." He hesitated as he sat on the sofa. "Well, troubled. Not quite the picture of a joyous bride-to-be I expected."

Pastor always seemed able to sense her moods in a strange way. She sighed and nodded. "I guess I am troubled. More than I've admitted to anyone else. And I don't *want* to be! This is for the best—I'm sure of it."

"I detect some trepidation in your manner. Are you trying to convince me or yourself?" Pastor Stevens pushed his heavy black hair away from his forehead. "Have you prayed about it?"

Sarah lifted her chin mutinously. "Not really. And

I know you're going to say I should. But God didn't seem to be listening all those months when I prayed for Rand's safety." She looked down at her hands.

Pastor Stevens frowned as he leaned forward. "I had a feeling you blamed God for Rand's death. I'm glad you're finally admitting it." He took her hand, his blue eyes warm with concern and compassion. "Sarah, please listen to me. It's hard, I know, but we can't always see God's plan in our lives. I remember when I was a little boy, lying on the floor at my grandmother's feet. She was doing some embroidery work, and I looked up at the underside of the hoop. The yarn was all tangled and gnarled. A real mess. But when I climbed up beside her and looked down at what she was working on, it was a beautiful garden. That's the way our lives are. We're looking at the picture from underneath, but God is working out a specific plan from above."

"No plan could be right without Rand in it. I don't care whose it is!" She didn't care if the words shocked her pastor. It was how she really felt. If God really loved her, he wouldn't let her go through this heartache.

Pastor Stevens got up and knelt beside Sarah's

chair. "God loves you, Sarah. He didn't promise we'd never have trouble or heartache. In fact, the Bible tells us we will. But he's given us his Word to go with us every step of the way. Can't you just trust him like you used to? I remember the old Sarah and how she believed God for every little thing in her life. Wouldn't you like to be that same young woman again?"

"I just can't!" She stood and moved to the window, her back to the pastor. "Maybe someday when the wounds aren't still so fresh, I'll be able to trust him like I should. But nothing has turned out like I expected. Every time I see the knoll on the other side of the woods, I'm reminded of the spot where Rand and I meant to build our home. Everywhere I look are reminders of how my life is in shambles."

She turned abruptly. "If you don't mind, Pastor, I have a lot of things to finish up." She knew she sounded rude, but she just couldn't talk about it anymore. It hurt too much.

He stood with reluctance, frustration etched on his face. "If you need to talk, you know where to find me. Please pray about this before you go through with it, Sarah."

She didn't answer him, and he left after gazing at

her for a moment. She breathed a sigh of relief when she heard the front door shut. She pushed away a stab of guilt as she went to the kitchen to start supper. She'd chosen her course, and she'd stick with it.

THREE

The train shrieked a warning of imminent arrival, and Rand Campbell jerked awake, his heart pounding. He licked dry lips—how he'd love a drink of his ma's iced tea. The thought of sun tea brewing in a glass jug on the back step at home caused a fresh wave of homesickness to wash over him. It wouldn't be long, though.

Then the fear he'd tried to keep at bay for the past three days flooded back. What would he find at home? He'd passed mile after mile of war-ravaged scenes.

Homes burned to the ground, fences torn down, hopeless looks on the faces of women and children. What if he arrived and found his home gone and his family missing? And Sarah. What if she was dead? What if she didn't wait for him? He pushed the thought away impatiently. His Sarah would wait no matter what. But then why didn't she write? Why hadn't his mother written? The unanswered questions made him feel sick.

The train whistle blew again, and he peered out the soot-streaked window. He was almost home. Eagerly, he scanned the rolling pastures. There was the Johnson place looking as neat and well-tended as usual. The Larsen farm looked unharmed. The train slowed as it began its descent into the valley. Through clearings in the lush canopy of glowing leaves, he could see the town just beyond.

The town of Wabash nestled between two steep hills, with the courthouse on the far hill overlooking the sprawling brick and wood buildings clustered neatly below it. He drank in the familiar buildings and the glimmer of water that ran in front of the town like a silver ribbon. During the heyday of the Wabash-Erie Canals, the river bustled with boats of all types and sizes, but since the railroad came, the canal traffic slacked off, and the river once again resumed its placid course.

Hungrily he watched for a familiar face. But the streets and boardwalks were almost deserted. The few people hurrying along were strangers, mostly women. So many men lost their lives in the war.

But the town looked just the same. There was Beitman & Wolf's. And Martha's Millinery, her fly-speckled window crowded with bonnets. Several old-timers in bib overalls lounged outside Lengel's Gun Shop.

Did the younger members of town still patronize the Red Onion Saloon? He grinned at a memory of the last ruckus he'd gotten into at the saloon, much to his grandma's dismay. She was always quoting Proverbs to him after an escapade at the Red Onion.

Those Bible verses he'd memorized at her knee were one of the things that got him through the horror of prison camp. Between starvation, dysentery, and murderous gangs, he'd watched a third of the men in camp die. He didn't really understand some of the verses very well, but they were somehow comforting. Maybe when his life settled down a little, he could study the Scriptures for himself.

His smile faded. The war had changed him and not for the better. Was there a way to get past the horrors he'd seen? He pushed his grandmother's memory away and gazed out the window intently.

The train gave one final, wheezing bellow, then came to a shuddering stop under the overhang of the depot. Rand took a deep breath and stood, pulling his haversack out from under his seat. Wouldn't it be grand if Pa or Jacob were in town? No chance of that, though. For one thing, he was here a good week earlier than he'd written he'd be. Lot more likely to find them in the field on the way home, if Jacob was even here. *And if he survived the war.*

His weak leg, injured by a bayonet, gave out as he stepped down, and he fell into an elderly, stooped man. "Why, I-I cain't believe it! Rand Campbell, is it really you?" Liam Murphy had worked at the train station for as long as Rand could remember. He grabbed Rand by the shoulders and peered into his face.

His hair was even more grizzled than Rand remembered, and his breath stank of garlic. Rand suppressed a grin. Liam's wife believed in garlic's medicinal qualities, so most folks steered clear of her specialties at the church picnics. "It's me all right, Liam."

"Rand," the old man gasped again before enfolding him in a bear hug. "We heard you was dead, boy."

Rand hugged him back until his words penetrated, then drew back in shock. "What do you mean, dead? I wrote my folks and Sarah every few weeks. I've been in the hospital in Washington, D.C."

Liam pulled a filthy handkerchief from his pocket and wiped his face with a shaking hand. "Wait till Myra hears 'bout this!" He put the dirty cloth back in his pocket. "Don't know nothing about no letters. No one here got no letters, I'm sure. Your folks been grieving themselves to death over you. Had a memorial service at church for you last spring, and I ain't never seen so many people at one of them things." He stared in Rand's puzzled face. "I'm telling you—we all thought you was dead!"

Rand felt like he'd been punched in the stomach. He couldn't catch his breath. How could something like this have happened? "I-I sent a letter with Ben Croftner to give to Sarah," he stammered. "Didn't he make it back here?"

A look of surprise and something else Rand couldn't identify flickered across Liam's face. "Yeah, he got back—let's see. Must be pert near five months ago." He paused and glanced at Rand. "But he didn't say nothing about no letter."

Something was odd in Liam's manner. "What aren't you telling me?" He fixed his eyes on the old porter's face.

The man flushed. "Well, now—I-I guess you have to hear it sooner or later," he stammered. "Ben's supposed to marry Sarah tomorrow. Right after church. Whole town's been invited. Ben's been strutting around all important-like."

The strength left Rand's knees, and he sat on the passenger bench outside the depot. The implications of what Liam said began to sink in, along with the bitter knowledge of Ben's betrayal. "I thought he was my friend. He let her go on thinking I was dead." He stood and slung his haversack over one broad shoulder, then turned south and strode off without saying good-bye to Liam, his slight limp more pronounced because of his fatigue.

Rand clamped down on the rage that was building in him. How could Ben do such a thing? And Sarah. How could she be so fickle? Why, he must have been declared dead only a few months before she took up with Croftner! Was that all the time she mourned someone she was supposed to love? His emotions felt raw, and he just couldn't seem to make any sense out of it.

By the time he made his way to the livery stable, paid for a horse, and swung up into the saddle, he was shaking with fury. He patted the mare's neck and set off toward home.

Being astride a horse again for the first time in a year cleared his thoughts, and he was more in control of his emotions by the time he pulled the mare off the road and headed up the deeply rutted track that followed the river. To gather his thoughts, he let the horse graze in the knee-high grass along the dirt track. He'd have Shane return the rental horse to the livery. His own horse, Ranger, would be glad to see him. He sat a moment and gazed out at Campbell land. The fields were tawny with drying corn. Harvest would be in a few weeks.

He turned the horse's head and urged her up onto the road again. They rounded the corner, and his heart quickened as the white two-story home on the hill overlooking the river came into view. Home. How he'd longed for this moment.

He pulled the horse up sharply. Should he go home first or see Sarah and demand an explanation? He could just see the roof of the large Montgomery house over the next rise. He let the horse prance on the path for a moment as he decided what to do.

No. He dug his heels into the mare's flank and turned up the Campbell lane. His family first. At least they'd mourned for him.

By the time he reached the front yard, his heart pounded and his palms were slick with sweat. A nagging headache persisted just behind his eyes. He pulled his horse to a stop and dismounted, a little disappointed no one was outside. He guided the horse to the shade of a big oak tree and tied her where she could reach the grass.

As he approached the back door, through the window he could see his mother washing dishes. A wave of love welled up in him as he saw the new gray in her hair and the fine web of wrinkles at her eyes. He breathed in the familiar scent of apple pie baking in the oven as he quietly opened the door.

His mother's back was to him, and he watched her a moment as she picked up a dish and proceeded to wash it. "I think I heard a horse," she said to the little brown dog lying on the rug by her feet. "Probably one of the menfolk home."

The little dog pricked her ears and whined as she

looked toward the door. His mother dipped the soapy plate in the pan of rinse water and laid it to drain on the wooden chopping block beside her.

Rand let the screen door bang behind him, but she didn't turn. "Don't bang the door," she said. Jody yipped and launched herself in a frenzy toward the door. His mother wiped her soapy hands on her apron and turned. Her eyes went wide as her gaze swept over him, then returned to lock with his.

"Ma." Rand knelt and picked up the little dog as he stared at his mother.

She froze, and Rand saw one emotion after another chase across her face. Uncertainty, disbelief, hope. She clutched her hands in the folds of her apron.

"Ma, I'm home." Rand patted Jody and laughed as the dog wriggled in his arms and licked his face joyously.

Her mouth opened, but no sound emerged as she stared at him.

"It's me, Ma."

"Rand?" she whispered as she took a faltering step toward him. "Rand!" With a noise something between a cry and a croak, she threw herself into his arms as the tears started down her cheeks.

Rand inhaled the aroma of her sachet, something

sweet with a rose scent. He struggled not to let the moisture burning his eyes slide down his cheeks. Home. He was finally home.

"Let me look at you." She held him at arm's length, then hugged him, laughing and crying as Jody whined and wagged her tail joyfully.

Rand clutched his mother so tightly he was afraid he hurt her. Ever since he was captured, he'd longed for his ma's gentle touch on his brow. At night when he awoke bathed in sweat from the pain, he had ached to lay his head on her breast and hear her soothing voice as she sang to him. He had been so hurt and bewildered at her silence after his release. Every time the door to the hospital ward opened, he had expected to see her anxious face.

"We thought you were dead."

"I know. There's a lot to tell you. How about some coffee?"

Jacob stopped short when he saw the strange horse munching grass in the shade. "You expecting any-one?" He shot a quizzical look at Shane and his pa.

Jeremiah shook his head. "Looks like that new bay from Larson's Livery. Must be someone from out of town."

They turned their horses over to one of the hands, then headed toward the kitchen door. A low murmur of voices drifted out the screen door, and Jacob paused. It almost sounded like Rand. But he knew better than to fall for that trick of his mind. There were times when he thought he caught a glimpse—out of the corner of his eye—of Rand in his favorite red plaid flannel shirt, striding past. He pushed into the kitchen as a dark-haired man, dressed in a blue Union uniform, rose from the kitchen table and turned to face him.

"Jake."

Rand had coined his nickname, and no one said it quite the way he did. Jacob opened his mouth to question this smiling, dark-eyed stranger who looked like—but of course couldn't be—Rand.

"Rand!" Shane flung himself past Jacob into Rand's waiting arms. A moment later all four men were hugging and slapping one another on the back, unashamed of the tears streaming from their eyes.

"The good Lord answered our prayers after all." With a shaking hand, Pa wiped at his eyes with his bandanna. He was breathing hard, as if he'd just run all the way from the back pasture to the house.

They sat around the kitchen table as Ma hurriedly poured them each a cup of coffee and joined them. Just as she sat down, the front door slammed.

Hannah, the eldest and the only girl, hurried into the kitchen. "Sorry I'm late, Ma." She stopped and looked at the group clustered around the table. Her puzzled stare stopped when her gaze met Rand's. She opened and closed her mouth several times, but no sound escaped.

"What! My gabby sister with nothing to say?" Rand stood, a teasing light in his eyes.

Hannah screamed and dropped the basket she was holding. Potatoes rolled across the wooden floor, and she almost tripped on them as she rushed toward her brother. She threw herself into Rand's arms, and he nearly toppled over.

"Careful," he said. "I'm still not quite myself."

She held him at arm's length. "Explain how this happened."

She hung onto his arm as he limped back to the table and sat down. "I was just about to tell Ma when you so rudely interrupted." He grinned. "Of course, that's nothing new—you've never learned how to be quiet."

"Very funny!" She punched him on the arm and sat beside him.

"Ouch." He rubbed his arm, then turned his grin at his family. "I was captured in northwest Georgia in September of '63. I'd been on reconnaissance, trying to see where the heaviest troop concentrations were. That's how I spent most of the war, slipping back and forth through enemy lines. The Rebs took me to Andersonville prison camp—"

"Andersonville!" Jacob shuddered, remembering the newspaper reports. "That camp is notorious. I heard the Union army found twelve thousand graves there when the war was over. They liberated it last May. You've been free for five months."

Rand nodded. "I was lucky I wasn't one of them. You can't imagine how bad it was. We had to build our own shelters, usually just a lean-to made with whatever we could find. Blankets, clothing, sticks. Some of the men could only dig a hole in the ground and cover up with a thin blanket. There were so many of us we just barely had enough space to lie down. And the food—"

He broke off and took a deep breath. "Well, it wasn't like yours, Ma. We were lucky if they gave us a little salt, maybe a half a cup of beans, and about a cup of unsifted cornmeal. Death was welcome for most of those guys. I helped bury over a hundred bodies in a common grave." His face was white.

Ma laid a trembling hand on his arm. "I just thank God you survived it, son."

He covered her hand with his. "I was delirious by the time we were freed. The doctor said I had dysentery and malnutrition." He smiled grimly. "I weighed less than a hundred pounds when I was brought to the hospital. A skeleton really. I've spent the last five months at Harewood General Hospital in Washington, D.C., recuperating."

"Why didn't you write?" Hannah burst out.

"I did. At least once a month."

Jacob shook his head. "We never received a single letter. Just a notification from the army of your death." He looked at his mother. "You want to show him, Ma?" He felt an inexplicable need to explain their willingness to believe Rand dead.

"I have it right here." Their mother hurried from the room and returned moments later waving a paper.

"See, right here." She thrust it under Rand's nose. "Official notice."

Rand studied it a moment, then handed it back. "There was a lot of confusion in the camps. It's not uncommon for this to happen."

"I knew you weren't dead. I just knew it," Shane put in excitedly. "I told Sarah just last week!"

At the mention of Sarah's name, Jacob's gaze went to his brother. He'd been dreading telling Rand about Sarah. He wouldn't take it well.

Rand stared back at Jacob, his eyes no longer smiling. "What about Sarah, Jake?"

Jacob started, then forced himself to look in his brother's hurt eyes. *He knew.* "What have you heard?"

"I already know she's going to marry Ben Croftner. How could she do that—didn't she mourn me at all?"

"Mourn you? You idiot!" Hannah stood and raked a hand through her mane of chestnut hair. "We all feared for her sanity! She refused to eat for days. Even now she hardly smiles. And you know what a perky, bubbly little thing she always was."

"Then why is she marrying Ben?"

Hannah hesitated, her gaze searching her brother's face. "William is dying." She sat back down beside her brother and took his hand. "Wade has her convinced that marrying Ben will help her father through this tough time. But that wily Ben has promised Wade that fifty acres of prairie he's always coveted as a marriage settlement."

"Hannah, you shouldn't gossip."

"It's not gossip, Ma. Rachel told me. Wade's taken advantage of Sarah's apathy since the news of your death to convince her. She thinks she owes it to the family to do this."

"Wade's always thought of himself instead of his family." Rand's voice was tight. "But there's something else you don't know." He stood and paced over to the window at the front of the kitchen, then wheeled to face them. "Ben has known all along I wasn't dead."

"What!" Their mother stood, her hand on her chest. "Are you sure?"

He nodded grimly. "Ben was with the troops who liberated the prison. I gave him a letter to give to Sarah."

Ma bit her lip. "Maybe he thought you died after he left."

Jacob clenched his fists. He wanted to find Croftner and pummel him. "He knew we read it in the paper last fall. And that we received an official notification shortly after that. I'm positive he never gave Sarah any letter."

"What about all the letters I wrote from the hospital?" Rand sat down and stretched his leg out in front of him.

"Maybe they were lost," Pa said. "The mail service has been wretched."

"All of them?" Rand shook his head. "Not likely. Ben must have gotten hold of them somehow."

"Labe works in the post office."

Shane's announcement silenced everyone. Finally Hannah spoke in a soft, hesitant voice. "Surely Labe wouldn't tamper with the mail." But her tone indicated her own doubt.

Jacob tried to tamp down his anger. "What other explanation is there, Sis?"

Rand got to his feet. "I'm going to see Sarah. Then I'm going to get to the bottom of this."

Ma held out a placating hand. "Let it go for now, son. Try to get a handle on your anger before you talk to Ben."

Rand shook off her hand. "Let it go? After all I've been through, you want me to let it go? Ben needs to find out he can't treat a Campbell like that."

Ma touched Rand's cheek. "What's gotten into you?" She paused, searching his face. "You've always been the even-tempered, rational one in the family."

"What do you expect, Ma? For me to just forget how Ben lied to and deceived the people I love? Well, I just can't do it. Maybe if I hadn't been through so much the last few years, I could. But I thought Ben was my friend. I trusted him. I deserve an explanation for what he's done."

"'Vengeance is mine; I will repay, saith the Lord,'" she quoted softly.

Rand stepped away, shaking his head. Jacob fell into step with him. "I'm going with you."

FOUR

Tomorrow she would be Mrs. Ben Croftner.

Sarah took a sip of tea and tried to drag her attention back to Myra Murphy's conversation, but her thoughts kept whirling around. The last few days had swept by in a daze, and now her future hurtled toward her at breathtaking speed. The lighthearted chatter of her friends around her, the brightly patterned quilt still attached to the quilting frame, the gifts heaped beside her should have brought her joy, but she was numb to all feelings but dread. She didn't want to leave her home, her comfortable, predictable life. And how well did she really know Ben? What if her new life was so different she couldn't adjust?

Suddenly aware of a strange hush in the room, Sarah looked around at the other ladies. They all wore the same look of shock and disbelief. Sarah twisted around to face the door herself to see what could cause such consternation among her friends.

She blinked at the figure blocking the sunlight as his broad shoulders spanned the doorway. Her gaze traveled up the gaunt frame to the face staring back at her intently. She gasped and began to rise to her feet. Was she dreaming? She put a hand to her throat. Her legs felt too weak to support her.

"Sarah."

The voice was so familiar, so beloved. She gasped, then took a step toward him and reached out a trembling hand.

Rand caught her hand. "Hello, Green Eyes." His gaze was as warm as a caress.

Her knees couldn't support her, and she clutched his hand, so warm, so real. She had to be dreaming. Hesitantly she reached up to touch his square jawline.

She felt the rough stubble on his chin. "Rand, it can't be, but it is. You're alive!"

She buried her face against his chest and inhaled his beloved, familiar scent. If it was a dream, she wanted never to awaken. But this was no dream. The rough texture of his uniform under her cheek, the familiar spicy tang of his hair tonic, and most important, the touch of his hands on her waist were all real.

Through a fog, she heard Jacob ask everyone to leave them alone. As soon as the door shut behind them, Rand pulled her away from his chest and she stared up into his brown eyes.

"Where have you been? We thought you were dead!" she whispered, blinking back tears.

"I know you were told I was dead. I stopped home first and Jacob told me." He pulled her back into his arms as if he couldn't bear to let her go.

She nestled against his chest again. This was where she belonged. How had she managed to go on breathing these past months? She sighed and lifted her head. "Tell me what happened."

He explained all the events of the past months while Sarah took in every detail of his appearance. He was too thin, but he looked grand in his blue uniform with the brass buttons gleaming and the cap perched on his dark hair. She shuddered as he described what he'd gone through in prison.

"I was so lost without you."

He stiffened, then picked up her left hand. The engagement ring Ben had given her only days before sparkled in the afternoon sun streaming through the lace curtains. "What about this, Sarah?" He dropped her hand and took a step back. "The thought of you waiting here—loving me, I thought—was the only thing that kept me alive during those long months at Andersonville. The only thing that kept me sane. Now I find you here with another man's ring on your finger."

"But, Rand, it's not what you think." She suddenly realized how bad this had to look to him. She reached toward him and he opened his arms, his expression anguished.

He embraced her for only a moment, then pulled away again. "Sometimes I questioned why I was allowed to live when I saw all my friends die, but I knew it was because you were waiting on me. Depending on me to come back to you. Did our love mean so little to you?"

His voice went hoarse. "I don't know what to think, Sarah."

"We-we thought you were dead," she whispered. "Don't you understand?"

"All I understand is that you forgot me in only a few short months."

"It's not like that. I'll break off the engagement immediately. You have to let me explain how it happened. I don't love him."

He continued to stare at her with a dark sorrow in his eyes. "Your wonderful new fiancé knew all along I wasn't dead."

She shook her head. "No, Rand, he told me—"

He began to pace, his limp becoming more prominent with every step. "He knew, Sarah. I gave him a letter to give to you. Did you get a letter?"

"No, but there must be some mistake. Ben cried when he told me about how he found your body—"

He wheeled around and shook his head. "He lied, Sarah." His voice was soft as if he were trying to make a child understand.

"Bu-but Ben *saw* your body." She felt idiotic repeating herself, but she couldn't seem to reconcile the two totally different stories.

"He was with the troops who liberated the prison, Sarah."

"But we saw in the paper—"

"It was wrong and he knew it was wrong. And how do you explain the letter he neglected to give you? A letter I personally put in his hands." Then he was in front of her, his hands warm on her shoulders. "You said you don't love him. Then why are you marrying him?"

"If I couldn't have you, at least I could make everyone else in my family happy. It seemed noble somehow. Papa wanted me settled before h-he dies. The doctor says he doesn't have long." His breath, so familiar and dear, caressed her face. She reached up and touched the stubble on his face again. "Oh, Rand, this is all too much to take in. I'm sure Ben didn't know."

But a dawning horror spread through her limbs. There were many dark layers to Ben, layers she hadn't wanted to poke into too deeply.

Rand's hands dropped away and he stepped back, his eyes hollow and desperate. "I can't believe you're defending him! I've written you and my folks many times while I was recuperating in Washington. You didn't get any of those letters either. And you know why? Labe works at the post office!" He took off his army hat and raked a hand through his thick hair.

What a fool she'd been. How gullible she was. All that phony sympathy—and the details he'd offered to prove to her Rand was really dead. "But we didn't know!"

Rand took a deep breath. "I didn't expect to have to argue you into believing me. I didn't think you'd defend what he's done. I have to think about this, Sarah." He gave her one last tortured glance before he turned toward to the door and stalked out.

"Rand!" she cried after his retreating figure. "Don't go. I do love you!" She ran after him, but he continued down the porch steps. "Wait. Please, wait." She caught his arm, but he shrugged it off and swung up onto Ranger's back.

He gazed down at her, the muscles in his throat working. "Maybe we can talk again in a few days. I just can't right now." He took a deep breath, then his jaw hardened. He shook his head slightly as though to clear it, dug his heels into the gelding's flank, and turned down the lane.

Jacob stepped from the porch where he'd been waiting and touched her shoulder. "Give him some time, Sarah. It will be all right." He went to his horse and swung into the saddle, then rode after his brother.

She stared after them in horror and disbelief. He had to listen to her—he just had to. She sank onto the porch step and buried her face in her hands. The ring Ben had given her just last week was a little too big, and it scratched her cheek where it had twisted toward her palm. The pain sharpened her senses, and everything was heightened. The color of the sky, the scent of autumn in the air. With Rand's reappearance, the numbness encasing her was gone, melted away.

Her senses vibrating, she stared at the ring on her finger. She wrenched it off and threw it as hard as she could toward the woods. She could see it winking in the sunlight as it arced up, then disappeared into the burnished canopy of leaves.

The buckboards and buggies were gone, and the house was quiet when she walked listlessly back inside. The ladies had all discreetly gone home, but the clutter left from the bridal shower was still strewn about the parlor. Rachel had left to go pick up Wade in town. Sarah kicked aside a box and sat down.

She felt numb, drained. There had to be some way to make Rand see, but she was just too tired to find it right now. But at least he was alive. What a wonderful miracle. She curled up on the sofa, her knees drawn up to her chest. She was so very tired. When she woke up she'd think of some way to get through to Rand.

FIVE

Rand paused for a moment on a knoll overlooking the Campbell home sprawling below him. He had so many conflicting emotions. His love for Sarah told him to forgive her and understand the situation, but his overwhelming disappointment just wouldn't let him. Everything was so different than he'd expected. He'd always thought her love was the kind that came along only once in a lifetime. And to find out now that she'd promised to marry Ben while he lay near death was just too much to take in.

"Wait up," Jake said from behind him.

Rand reined in his horse and waited for his brother. "I'm going to town."

"To see Ben?"

"You got it." He wheeled Ranger toward Wabash. He was reasonably certain where Ben could be found too. Unless he'd changed a lot, he'd be at the back table at the Red Onion. Ben was certainly going to be surprised when Rand walked in. Or maybe not. Maybe he had read his letters before he destroyed them.

They rode silently toward town, the stillness broken only by the clopping of the horses' hooves and the croaking of the frogs along the riverbank. The fecund smell from the river wafted in on the breeze.

"You know where Ben lives?" Rand asked.

"He bought that fancy brick house on Main Street. You know the one Judge Jackson built?"

Rand lifted a brow and glanced at his brother. "How'd he ever afford a place like that?"

"Land speculation, mostly. And investments since he got back, I guess. He's pretty closemouthed about it. I'll show you. If he's not there, we'll head for the Red Onion."

Rand followed his brother as they cantered up the

steep Wabash Street hill and turned down Main Street, dimly illuminated by gaslights. The house loomed over the street, its brick turrets and high peaks grander and more lavish than any of its neighbors.

The men approached the paneled walnut doors, and Rand pounded on the door with his fist, not bothering with the brass knocker. No one answered, and he pounded again.

"I don't think anyone is home," Jacob said.

"We'll catch up with him at the tavern." Rand spun his horse around and cantered for town.

Sarah awoke as the clock chimed, reminding her how late it was. She hurriedly threw more wood into the cookstove and sat at the table to snap green beans. Papa and Joel would be back from town anytime, and Wade, demanding supper, wouldn't be far behind with Rachel. There was a heavy cloud cover, and the smell of rain came through the open window. It was already dark, although it was barely six o'clock.

"Sarah."

She jumped at the sudden sound. She had been

so lost in thought she hadn't heard the knock on the door. Ben had walked into her home as if nothing were amiss. "How dare you come here after what you've done! How could you do such a thing to me—to Rand's family?"

"Rand, always Rand! Don't you care about my feelings at all?" He reached out and swept a vase from the table. His gaze snapped to her bare left hand. "Where's your ring?" He grasped her shoulders and squeezed.

Sarah stared at him. "You think I would marry you after all you've done?" His grip hurt her arms. "After you lied and tricked me? You're not the man I thought you were at all."

Ben ignored her retort. "Where—is—your—ring?" He punctuated every word with a shake, and her hair tumbled out of the pins and down her back.

"I threw it into the woods," she said with a defiant toss of her head.

His fingers bit deeper into the soft flesh of her arms, and she winced. "Do you have any idea how much that ring cost?" he shouted.

"Is money all you care about? Don't you care about the pain you've caused?" She couldn't believe how quickly his tender, well-mannered facade crumbled.

He seized her elbow and yanked her toward the door.

"What are you doing?" Panicked, Sarah tried to free herself. "Let go of me!" The fabric ripped under her elbow as she tried to wrench her arm out of his grip.

"You're mine, Sarah, and no one else's. You're coming with me." He hauled her struggling form through the door and hoisted her up beside Labe, waiting in the buckboard, the brim of his hat pulled low to shield his face from the misty rain just beginning to fall.

Labe's face was pale, and his mouth worked soundlessly. "I'm sorry, Sarah," he finally whispered as he tied her hands together with a piece of rough rope. "I tried to talk him out of this, but there was no stopping him."

"Shut up," his brother snarled as he crawled up beside Sarah. "Everything arranged?"

Labe nodded uncertainly. "Bedrolls are in the back, along with everything else you said."

The glint in Ben's eyes made her gut twist. Was he insane? With renewed fear, she lunged backward, intending to crawl over the bedrolls and out the back, but Ben was too quick for her.

He sat her back in the seat with a bone-jarring thump. "If you don't sit still, I'll truss you up like a chicken."

And he would too. She could see it in his eyes. Shivering from the cold needles of rain that pelted down in earnest now, she huddled in the seat and tried to think of how to get out of this mess.

"You don't need to tie her, Ben." Labe touched her arm, then untied the ropes. "She won't cause no trouble, will you, Sarah?"

She shook her head but couldn't bring herself to lie. She'd jump off this buckboard the moment she could.

Ben picked up the reins, but before he could slap them against the horse's flank, two riders came around the curve of the lane. He squinted in the near darkness. Then his eyes widened.

"Rand!" Sarah cried in relief. She started to clamber over Labe, but Ben grabbed her arm.

"Let go of her, Ben. This is between you and me." Rain dripping from the broad brim of his army hat, Rand slid to the ground and walked toward the buckboard, skirting the widening mud puddles. Jacob followed close behind.

The click as Ben drew back on the hammer of his revolver was muffled in the pattering rain. "Don't come any closer, Campbell."

Rand stopped. "Why'd you do it, Ben? Why lie to everyone?"

Ben's face twisted. "Don't talk to me about lies. You're the biggest liar there ever was." He scoffed. "What a fake. My pa thought the sun rose and set with you. No-account drunk that he was, always getting into scrapes when the liquor got the best of him. I bet you don't even remember the time you stopped and helped him mend our fence and round up the escaped cattle. Like I couldn't have done that if he'd have just asked me. But no, it was always, 'Ben, why can't you be like that Campbell boy?'"

He aimed the gun at Rand. "And then there was Sarah. She mooned over you for years, but did you pay her any notice? No. Even though she was the prettiest girl in Wabash. But just as soon as she took a notice of me, you had to have her. *My* girl."

"I was never your girl!" Sarah's gaze never left his gun.

Ben continued as if he didn't hear her. "When I got back from the war and they all thought you were dead, I knew fate was finally smiling on me. Sarah would be mine. But you had to come back early and spoil everything, just like you always have. Well, you're not going to ruin things for me ever again." He brought the revolver up with sudden determination and fired.

Just as he pulled the trigger, Sarah leaned against him with all her might, and the shot went wild. "Run, Rand!"

But instead of running, Rand launched himself at Ben and dragged him off the buckboard seat. The two men thrashed in the mud and the muck. Rand threw a hard right swing that connected solidly with Ben's cheek. Ben reeled back and hit his head on the wheel of the buckboard as he fell.

Rand pushed his hair out of his eyes and stepped away from Ben. "Is he dead?"

Sarah stared at Ben's pale face and saw him draw a ragged breath. "No." Shivering and soaked to the skin, she climbed awkwardly out of the buckboard on rubbery legs and almost fell as she reached toward Rand. "Thank God you're all right!"

"What were you doing with Ben, Sarah?"

She looked at the scene: a carriage packed as if ready for a journey. She imagined how it must seem to Rand, who'd just learned he'd been deceived on what should have been a happy day of reunion. She stared at him in dismay. Surely he didn't think she was running off with Ben willingly?

She raised her chin. "Ben saw that I'd taken off his ring and dragged me out to the carriage. He'd have kidnapped me if you and Jacob hadn't shown up."

"Is that so?"

She caught his arm again. "Rand, surely you don't believe—"

His eyes hooded, he turned away.

Jacob nudged Ben with his boot. "I think one of us had better ride after Doc Seth. Ben doesn't look too good."

"I'll go." Rand shook off Sarah's restraining hand and mounted his horse. "You keep an eye on Croftner."

She stood looking after him. He had to listen to her eventually. He just had to.

SIX

Rand sensed Sarah's gaze on his back as she stood beside Doc Seth, but he resisted looking at her. The rain had soaked through every scrap of his clothing, and he shivered as a buggy came sloshing around the corner. When it stopped, a slight, frail figure slowly clambered down.

"William?"

Sarah's father turned as Rand stepped out from the shadows. Tears started to fill William's eyes as he opened his arms and drew Rand into an embrace. "My dear boy, I heard the news in town. What a happy day this is for all of us."

William had always been frail but vibrant in spite of it all. Rand didn't recognize him in this stoop-shouldered man with deep lines of pain around his mouth. The older man's fragility reminded him of a dying baby bird he'd found once, its bones thin and brittle.

"It-it's good to see you, sir," he stammered, trying to hide his dismay.

"You too, son. You too." William drew back and wiped his eyes shakily with his handkerchief. "What's going on here?"

"I gather that Ben was trying to force Sarah to go off with him." Rand explained Ben's deception.

"This is all so much to take in. When the war ended, it seemed the horrors would at last come to an end. Now it seems they're piling up even in times of peace." William shook his head.

Doc Seth straightened and stepped over to Rand and William. "He'll live, but he's sure going to wake up with a sore head. Labe can take him home and put him to bed, and I'll look in on him tomorrow." He thrust out a hand to Rand. "Good to have you home, young Campbell. Amelia told me the news."

Rand shook his hand. "Tell her I'll stop by and see her soon." He broke off, and they all turned as another horse and buggy cantered into the yard.

Wade slid down from his buggy, his face florid. "What's going on here?" He didn't bother to help his wife down but stomped over to where his father stood.

Joel slid down from the buggy and bounded into Rand's arms. "Rand! Oh, Rand!"

Rand laughed and hugged him tightly. He loved Sarah's little brother as much as his own. "How you doing, half-pint?"

"Great! I've missed you so much. When can we go fishing?"

Rand grinned at the familiar question. He'd always felt sorry for the lad. William's health prevented much of the usual father-son relationship, and Wade wasn't much of a fisherman. He'd started taking Joel fishing when he was two. "Soon."

He pulled a hand free and thrust it out for Sarah's older brother. "Good to see you, Wade." It wasn't really, but he could at least make an attempt at civility.

Wade ignored the outstretched hand. "You beat up my sister's fiancé and think you can just sit on our porch like an old friend? Why aren't you in jail?"

Rand lowered his hand and put it back in his pocket. What was there to say in the face of such animosity? Wade always saw things his own way.

"That's enough!" William's voice boomed out in a sudden surge of strength. "Your treatment of a guest in our home is unacceptable, Wade. You have no idea of the wrong that's been done to him over the past few months."

Wade glared at his father, his massive hands clenched. "So he was a prisoner of war. Lots of men were. He can't just show up here as if we're all going to bow and scrape and give up all we've worked for to accommodate him. Sarah, get inside. We have a wedding to prepare for."

His father lifted a brow. "You know as well as I do that Sarah would never marry Ben now."

Wade's color deepened. "How do you know her feelings haven't changed? Ben would make a much better husband than Campbell."

"Why, because he's rich? A man who could deceive her the way Ben has isn't worthy of my daughter."

William directed a slight smile Sarah's way. "Besides, she loves Rand. Always has, always will. Right, honey?"

Sarah nodded.

The muscles in Wade's jaw pulsed as he clenched his teeth. "But what about the land?"

"Is that all you care about? More land, more money?" William shook his head wearily. "I'm telling you right now, if you do anything to hurt Sarah or Rand, you won't have *this* land or house."

Wade stared at his father. "You'd cut me out of your will?"

"In a minute. Now get in the house until you can get a civil tongue in your head."

Wade shot a glance at Sarah, then swung his blistering gaze toward Rand before stomping into the house. He let the screen door slam shut behind him. Rachel sighed and followed him.

"Good for you, Papa." Sarah slipped her small hand into his.

"Wade's had it coming. I should never have let him get away with his arrogance for so long." William took his hat off and rubbed his forehead. The confrontation had drained him. "Come in out of the rain, sweetheart. You and Rand can have the parlor. I'm just going to have a bite to eat and go to bed." He shook Rand's hand. "Stop by tomorrow and we'll talk. I'm just as eager as Joel to hear the full story." He walked into the house, his shoulders stooped.

Sarah watched her father stumble up the steps and into the house. An order from Pa wouldn't stop Wade for long. Why did he hate Rand so? She shook her head. Ever since she could remember there had been antagonism between them. And Rand had tried. But every overture he'd made had been ignored or ridiculed.

She pushed the disturbing puzzle out of her mind and turned back to Rand. "Can we talk?"

"There's nothing to say right now." His tone was abrupt. "I still don't know how I feel about you or anything else." He took off his sopping hat and ran a weary hand through his wet hair.

"Campbell!" Ben's hoarse growl interrupted them. Glowering, he raised his head from the back of the buckboard. "This isn't over, Campbell. You'll never have her. Never. You just remember that." His head fell back against the floor of the buckboard as Labe slapped the reins against the horse's flank, but Ben watched them until he was out of sight, a burning hatred in his eyes.

Sarah shivered. "I think he means it. Watch your back, Rand."

"I can take care of myself. You're soaked to the bone. You go on in now. Just give me some time."

Sarah hesitated, her eyes searching his sober face. Time? How much time? But she left the questions unanswered and walked wearily up the porch steps, her wet skirt dragging in the mud. She turned to watch Rand and Jacob mount up and ride down the lane and around the curve. Didn't he realize how much time they'd wasted already?

❧

The next morning Rand woke disoriented. The familiar clanging of trays in the hallway and the squeak of nurses' shoes scurrying was missing. Sunshine streamed in the window and illuminated suddenly familiar surroundings. The toy soldiers Grandpa had carved for him when he was five were lined up on a battered chest against the wall. His fingers stroked the brightly colored quilt, soft and faded with numerous washings. The rug on the unpainted wood floor was as threadbare as he remembered it.

He glanced at the space next to him. Jacob was nowhere to be seen, but there was that indentation on the pillow, a sight he'd seen hundreds of times and had thought he'd never see again.

He jumped out of bed, eager to get downstairs. He wouldn't worry about anything today, he decided as he splashed cold water on his face. He was just going to enjoy being with his family again after three long years. No uniform either. He opened his closet, grabbed a pair of overalls and his favorite plaid shirt, and pulled them on. The pants hung around his waist, and they were too long, but they would have to do.

By the time he pulled on socks and boots, the aroma of coffee and ham filled the air and made his stomach rumble. The low murmur of voices quickened his steps as he hurried down the stairs.

His mother spun around as he stepped into the kitchen. "I was just coming to wake you. I fixed ham and eggs, grits, flapjacks, and coffee. I'll have you fattened up in no time." She gave him a quick, reassuring hug.

Rand grinned as he squeezed her, breathing in the faint fragrance of roses that clung to her. She wouldn't be Ma without that scent. He remembered gathering wild roses every summer for her to make sachets for her bureau drawers. He dropped his arms as she bustled over to the cookstove, then offered him a plate piled high with food. His mouth watered as he took it from her and sat between Shane and Jacob.

Hannah came hurrying in as Rand took his first sip of strong, hot coffee. Her face brightened as she saw Rand shoveling another forkful of eggs into his mouth. "Now I am sure it's really you." She slipped into the chair opposite him. "The brother I remember is always eating."

Rand, a wicked grin on his face, caught Jacob's eye and gave a meaningful nod. "How come you're still here, anyway, Sis? Thought you would have trapped yourself a husband by now."

"Come on, Rand. Be realistic." Jacob poked him with an elbow. "Who would have her? She has always been the ugliest Campbell."

Rand stared at his sister. "Yeah, I forgot about that big nose of hers. And all that hair."

"Not to mention her temper! Her tongue could cut a man to ribbons." Jacob grinned at the rising color on Hannah's face.

Rand knew they'd get a reaction when they hit on her sore spot. She was always moaning about her nose. Personally, Rand didn't see anything wrong with it, but she seemed to think it didn't match the pert ones described in her favorite novels.

She flushed a deep red, then burst into tears.

"Hey, I'm sorry, Sis." Rand hadn't expected this much of a reaction. He reached over and put an arm around her. "You know we were only teasing. I've always liked your nose."

Hannah just cried harder. "It's not that," she finally sputtered as Rand handed her his bandanna. She drew a deep breath. "It's just so wonderful to have you here, to see Jacob smile again, to hear your voice—" She stopped and gulped.

The dimples deepened in Rand's cheeks as he stared at his sister. "It sure is good to be home. To be with you all again just like before this crazy war ever happened. You don't know how anxious I was to get home. I was so scared when no one answered my letters."

Their parents had been watching the exchange between their children with indulgent smiles, and Ma's eyes welled with tears at Rand's words. She dabbed at her eyes with a lace-edged hankie.

His dad cleared his throat gruffly. "You're just in time to help with the farming too. It's almost more than Shane and I can handle. I've tried to talk your brother into staying home, but he won't listen. Now I'll have some help come spring."

Rand glanced at Jacob. Hadn't he told them of Rand's plans? He and his brother had lain awake for hours talking last night. He'd been hoping that by now Jacob would have broken the news to their father. His brother shook his head slightly.

Pa's gaze traveled from one son to the other. "What is it?"

Rand hated to disappoint their father. "I-I won't be able to stay long, Pa," he stammered. "I'm in the Third Cavalry. I can stay for about a week, but then I have to report for duty." He winced at the stricken look in his mother's eyes. "I've been garrisoned at Fort Laramie. I still have two years to go of my service."

"Not you too!" Hannah stood twisting her hands in her apron. "The Sioux have been rampaging for months out there. Isn't it bad enough we're losing Jacob?"

Jacob shrugged. "That's why so many of us are being sent out West. And I've found out in the past couple of years how much I enjoy the cavalry. I've always wanted to see the frontier, so I don't mind the assignment. Maybe I can find my own spread while I serve my country."

"Rand, no." His father rose to his feet. "Why do you think I've worked so hard on this farm? Always expanding, always looking for ways to make more money?" He put an arm around Ma. "It's been for you! For you and your brothers. You can't go! Surely the army would release you after all you've been through."

His mother flinched as the words echoed in the warm kitchen. He stood and faced his father. "I don't want to be released. I'm a grown man, Pa. This is what I want."

Ma laid a gentle hand on his arm. "Your pa is just concerned, Rand. Can't you think about staying home now and letting us all begin to heal? You can raise horses right here on land that's been in the Campbell family for twenty-five years instead of fighting Indians to gain a small piece of land in some godforsaken wilderness. You haven't been with us for three years."

His mother had always been able to change his mind in the past, and he fought against the soft persuasion in her voice. "I can't, Ma." He raked a hand through his hair. "I need to prove something to myself, to build my own dreams with my own sweat. I have to go."

Pa took a long look at his son's granite face, then left the room. Ma opened her mouth to try again, but one look at the firm set to Rand's mouth changed her mind.

Always the peacemaker, Hannah cleared her throat and laughed self-consciously. "So, the calvary, huh? You've always had the magic touch with horses and cattle. When Ma was carrying Jacob, she asked you if you wanted a baby brother or sister. You looked up with those brown eyes of yours all serious and said, 'If it's all the same to you, Ma, I'd just as soon have a horse.'"

Laughter defused the tension as they heard the familiar story. Jacob punched Rand in the arm. "Yeah, and you've been treating me like a beast of burden ever since!"

When the laughter faded, Hannah looked at Rand and said softly, "You are taking Sarah, aren't you?"

Rand looked away from her expectant face. "No." It was all he could do to shake his head, to stick to his decision. "Not right now. I need some time to accept all that's happened. I'll keep in touch, and down the road, we'll see if we can work things out." He folded his arms across his chest. "Anyway, that area is no place for a woman. She'd soon get sick of being confined to the fort. You know how independent she is."

"Jacob is taking Amelia. It must not be too dangerous."

Hannah's expression turned mutinous as she opened her mouth to argue further.

"Don't push me, Hannah. I know you're concerned, but I have to be sure in my own mind why she took up with Ben. She was mighty young when I left for the war—only sixteen. I need to be sure she knows her own mind."

Hannah sighed impatiently. "Why are men so thickheaded?" She rolled her eyes.

Rand grinned and pushed away from the table. "It's the only protection we have against you women." He stood and stretched. "Better get to the fields. I'll help all I can while I'm here."

"What about your leg?"

"I feel fine, Sis. And I need to work at getting my strength back." He grabbed his hat and followed his brothers out the door.

Out on the porch, Jacob stopped and thrust his

hands in his pockets. "Don't you know how rare it is to find someone to love the way you love Sarah? Don't throw it away."

Rand looked away. "Nothing was like I expected, Jake. Things turned out pretty well for you, though. You and Amelia. You'll be married and off on an adventure together."

"You could be, too, if you weren't so pigheaded." Jacob's lips flattened, then finally curved into a smile. "Swallow your pride. Go see Sarah. She never stopped loving you. She pined for you. Haven't you even noticed how thin she is? If losing you once nearly destroyed her, what do you think losing you again would do to her? You'll come back and find her dead and buried."

Rand inhaled sharply at the thought. He stared into his brother's brown eyes and saw the certainty there. "It wouldn't hurt to just talk, I reckon."

Jacob clapped his hand on Rand's shoulder. "Then get to it. I can handle the plowing."

❧

Sarah sighed as she stared across the river. What could she do to change Rand's mind? She hadn't heard a word from him all day. Should she try to find him? But he'd said to give him some time. So she'd come to their favorite spot to wait him out. She leaned down and picked up a flat rock. She skimmed it across the water, and it skipped three times. Not very good. She was losing her touch. She reached down for another rock.

"The last time I saw you do that, it skipped six times."

She turned immediately and smiled. Rand. It was almost as if her hopeless wishing had conjured him up. "Oh, Rand, I'm so glad you came."

He held out his arms, and she rushed into them. The scent of his hair tonic slipped up her nose. A familiar scent that clouded her thoughts into a hopeless jumble.

She buried her face in his broad chest and clung until he lifted her chin. His brown eyes searched her face, and the touch of his breath on her cheek was like a caress. She'd waited so long for this. His mouth came down on hers, so tentative yet so familiar. As his lips touched hers, she wrapped her arms around his neck and kissed him back with all the love in her heart.

He pulled her closer, his right hand pressing her

waist. His passionate response convinced her she hadn't lost him after all. It would be all right. It had to be.

"I tried to stay away, Green Eyes, but I couldn't," he whispered. He loosed his grip on her with a sigh.

She refused to step away and clung to his shirt with both hands. "I'm so sorry about Ben." How did she even begin to explain?

"It's not your fault." He shook his head. "I realized it as soon as I cooled down enough to think. I can't blame you for wanting to go on with your life."

"You are my life. Nothing seemed real with you gone. I-I knew I couldn't be happy, so I thought if everyone else was happy, it would be enough." She swallowed hard, remembering the hopelessness of her future. "But I dreaded the very thought of marriage." She looked up at him.

"You're that opposed to marrying?" His dimple flashed.

The pressure in her chest increased. "Not to marrying the right man."

"And who would that be?" His voice held a teasing lilt she hadn't heard in so long.

"I think you know." The joy she felt inside almost couldn't be contained. "James Benson left on the wagon train last May, and his cabin is still empty. We can live there until our place is built on our knoll."

Rand's smile faded and he looked away. "I can't stay, Sarah. I'm still in the cavalry. I'm heading out West in a couple of days."

She inhaled and held her breath as his words soaked in. "Not staying here?" She stared at him. "But we've always planned to build on the knoll and help Papa with the farm. He's not well, Rand. I can't go running off out West and leave him. Besides, where else would we go?"

"I'm going West." He reached out and wrapped a strand of her hair around his finger. "Your pa will understand. He came here with your ma and settled just like I want to do. He wasn't content to stay in Philadelphia."

The very thought filled her with terror. "That was different. He was poor and had no prospects. You have land here, both mine and yours from your pa. Can't you ask to be released so you can heal?" She wanted to grab him and shake some sense into him. "Surely you're not serious about this scheme. We've made too many other plans."

"It's not different. Once my enlistment's over,

I don't want to take something another man built. There's so much opportunity out West, Sarah. Land for the taking, gold, new businesses." His dark eyes glowed, and he gripped her shoulders in his big hands. "It will be a great life. Besides, do you really think Wade and I could get along well enough to work together?"

"Rand." Panic stole her breath. "I couldn't leave Papa. You haven't seen how ill he's been. He seems to go downhill every day. It would kill him for me to leave."

He frowned. "I saw how poorly he looked. But Sarah, he would understand. He wouldn't want you to stop living because of him. Let's go ask him." He took her arm and started toward the house, but she pulled away.

"No! I don't want to upset him. I just can't go now. Can't you wait? Just until he doesn't need me? He doesn't have very long. The doctor said maybe a year."

"I have my orders and a letter to deliver for General Sherman. I have to go."

She took a deep breath and stepped back from him. "You can't ask me to sacrifice my father." Tears filled her eyes as she saw Rand's face fall. She *couldn't* leave Papa.

"I understand. I love your father too. Good-bye, Sarah. Have a good life." He turned and left her standing on the path.

She opened her mouth to call him back, but the words died in her throat. What was the use? She couldn't go and he wouldn't stay. It was as simple as that. He didn't really love her, or he wouldn't ask her to leave Papa. Not as sick as he was. Couldn't Rand see that? She grabbed a flat stone and hurled it toward the water. It skipped seven times and sank. But there was no one left to see.

A
HEART'S
OBSESSION

ONE

September 22, 1865

The town of Wabash, Indiana, bustled with activity as the horse's hooves clopped along the plank street and up the hill. Rand Campbell reined in the mare pulling the family buckboard and stopped in front of the train depot. The engine shrieked and puffed out a billow of soot that burned his throat as he, Jacob, and Shane climbed down. Now that the time had arrived for his departure, Rand wished he had been able to stay longer. Leaving his mother and father had been rough. Ma had cried, then pressed his grandma's Bible into his hand before hurrying away, and Pa wouldn't even come out of the barn to say good-bye.

Shane snuffled, and Rand ruffled his brother's blond hair, then hugged him. "I'm counting on you to take care of the family, squirt." Though at fifteen, the lad was eye level with Rand.

Shane bit his quivering lip and nodded, straightening his shoulders. He trotted around behind the buckboard, heaved the saddle over one shoulder, then led Ranger to the waiting train. Rand's horse would accompany him west.

Rand put his hand in his pocket. His fingers rubbed against a familiar round shape. He'd smuggled it into the prison in his shoe and had spent months sanding off the engraving on the golden eagle coin before chiseling his and Sarah's names into the gold.

His gaze swept the familiar sights of Wabash at the top of the hill. The whitewashed courthouse, the jail to the west of it, and the bustle of Commercial Row just down the steep Wabash Street hill made his heart ache at the thought of leaving. But knowing he'd never see Sarah again hurt the most.

He'd come home after his internment in Andersonville Prison to find his fiancée engaged to Ben Croftner. When things were sorted out and Ben's lies were exposed, Rand had hoped Sarah would go west with him, but she'd put her family above him. He'd taken that hurt and used it to build a wall around his heart.

He fingered the love token. What good would it do in his pocket? He'd never give it to anyone else because he'd never feel like this about anyone else. That kind of love was dead for him.

He pulled out the token and thrust it into Jacob's hand. "Give this to Sarah, Jake. Tell her I'm sorry it didn't work out and I hope she has a happy life."

Jacob's fingers closed around the token. "You make it sound like there's no hope for the two of you."

"There isn't. I wish it weren't so, but I doubt I'll see Sarah again." Rand hefted the haversack over his shoulder and picked up the hamper of food, then his satchel.

"All aboard!"

He was a cavalry man, and this was what he wanted—a life he made for himself, beholden to no one. After one last look at his brothers, he raced toward the plodding train and jumped up the steep steps. He caught one last glimpse of Jacob, standing with one arm upraised, his other arm around their younger brother, Shane. Rand waved until the buckboard with the two figures beside it was no longer in view, then took a deep breath and limped to a vacant seat. His great adventure was about to begin.

Sarah Montgomery sat on a rock along the banks of the Wabash River and listened to the train whistle blow as the engine left the station. The sun on this fine September day warmed her face. A robin, its red breast a bright flash of color, fluttered by to land on a nearby gooseberry bush. The bird swooped down to grab a worm. The rhythm of life went on even though her heart felt dead in her chest. She was only nineteen, but right now she felt like ninety.

How did she go on after losing Rand and then finding him again, only to watch him leave her without a thought? Time stretched in front of her, a lifetime spent without the man she'd loved since she was a girl. A vision of his dark hair and eyes resided in her heart and always would.

She picked up the book she'd brought with her, *A Christmas Carol*. The novel absorbed her until the sun moved lower in the sky. She closed it and glanced around to make sure she had all her belongings before going back to the house to start dinner.

"Sarah?"

She looked up to see Jacob, Rand's younger brother, approaching with a tentative smile. "He's gone?"

Jacob, dressed in his blue cavalry uniform, took off his wide-brimmed hat and turned it in his hands. "I'm sorry, Sarah. How you doing?"

Though her eyes burned, she was past tears. "I'll be fine." She tipped up her chin. "I have Papa and Joel to care for." She studied the compassion in Jacob's brown eyes. "D-Did he say anything about me?"

Jacob nodded and stepped closer. He pulled his hand from his pocket, and something metallic winked in the sunlight. "He asked me to give you this."

She rose from her perch on a rock and reached out to take it from him. Her fingers rubbed over the gold metal. "A love token." She choked out the words as she stared at the words engraved in the metal. *Rand and Sarah.*

"He worked on this in prison."

Her fingers traced the engraving. "Did he say anything about me joining him?"

Jacob's eyes held sympathy as he shook his head. "No, he didn't, Sarah. I'm sorry. H-He said to tell you he was sorry it didn't work out and he hoped you'd have a happy life."

The pain crushed in on her again. The good-bye was final, just like the one that loomed with her father. Her fingers closed around the coin, and the edges bit into her palm. "Thank you, Jacob. I'll treasure it."

Kansas City was a sprawling assortment of wooden shops and storefronts. The streets teemed with horses and cattle, buggies and buckboards. And people. Everywhere, people hurried across the muddy streets and crowded the uneven boardwalks. Rand felt invigorated by the hustle and bustle, despite the smell of manure and the distant lowing of cattle from the stockyards.

A broad-shouldered man shouting orders to his cowboys pushed past Rand with a brief tip of his hat. Rand stared after him. His stint in the cavalry would give him the opportunity to find his own spread. Someday he'd bring his own cattle to a stockyard like this one.

Across from the depot was the Holladay Stagecoach station, and he walked across the street and stood in line behind another soldier. "Heading to Fort Leavenworth, then on to Fort Laramie too?"

The other man turned with a grin on his open, friendly face. "Sure am. Been on leave and kinda hate to go back. You new?"

"Lieutenant Rand Campbell." He thrust out a soot-streaked hand.

"Lieutenant Isaac Liddle." He shook Rand's proffered hand, then took off his wide-brimmed hat and wiped his forehead with a bandanna. "What unit you with?"

"H Troop, Third Cavalry. You?"

"Third Battalion. You're going to like Old Bedlam. You heard of it?"

Rand shook his head, liking the looks of his companion. Isaac reminded him in some ways of Jacob. Though Isaac had auburn hair and a dusting of freckles, he had the same muscular build and quiet, friendly manner as Jacob. Strong, capable hands. A man you could depend on. And from what he'd heard of the Indian Wars, you wanted that kind of man around.

Isaac grinned. "It's what we call the single officers' quarters. It came by its name legitimate. A lot of loud shenanigans go on at all hours. At least I assume that's where you'll be quartered. I don't see a pretty lady with you. You're not married?"

"No." He pushed away an image of Sarah's heart-shaped face, long red-gold hair, and dancing green eyes.

"I was hopin'. Fort Laramie doesn't have many women right now." He put his hat back. "Where you from?"

"Wabash, Indiana. Born and raised on a farm about two miles out of town." Rand was grateful for the change in topic. "Where you hail from?"

"El Paso, Texas." Isaac held one hand out in front of him hastily when he saw Rand's eyebrows rise. "But I fought for the Union."

That explained his accent. The line moved forward, and Rand followed. "What's the status of the Indian Wars?"

Isaac frowned. "We got trouble brewing with Red Cloud. That's why so many are being sent out for reinforcements. They haven't attacked Laramie yet, but we have to send out troops even on woodcutting duty. Maybe it's a good thing you don't have a wife. She would be an added worry."

Jacob was bringing Amelia. Rand glanced toward the telegraph station. There was no time to send a telegram to his brother, though, and even if he did, Rand didn't see Amelia agreeing to stay behind. A frown on his face, he picked up his luggage, waved to Isaac, then went to the livestock car to get Ranger for the trek to Fort Leavenworth.

Rand's brass buttons and buckles glimmered in the sunshine, and Ranger's sleek black coat shone. He and his detachment met Major DuBois about three miles north of Fort Leavenworth. There was no mistaking the major. He sat on his black horse with stiff military bearing, and his uniform was precisely brushed and neat.

Rand saluted. "Good morning, sir. I'm Lieutenant Campbell, and I'm pleased to escort you to Fort Laramie." He'd been at Fort Leavenworth a week when he was ordered to meet a column and escort them on to Fort Laramie.

The major saluted smartly. "At ease, Lieutenant." He dismounted and motioned for Rand to do the same. "How's the situation with the Indians? Any trouble brewing?"

Rand dismounted and joined the major. "Nothing I can put my finger on, sir. But I have an uneasy feeling that something's brewing that we can't see right now. There have been grumblings about the miners tramping through the Sioux hunting grounds on the Bozeman Trail. Red Cloud hasn't come in for rations, and some of our tame Oglala Sioux say he's calling for a fight to the knife. I don't trust him."

The major waved his hand dismissively. "We'll deal with him if he steps out of line."

The flap to the ambulance behind them opened and a young woman stepped through the opening. "Good morning, Daddy. Why have we stopped? Have we arrived?"

Something about her reminded Rand of Sarah. Maybe it was the sweet smile she directed his way or the red in her hair. He waited to be introduced.

The major smiled. "Lieutenant, I'd like you to meet my daughter, Jessica. And my wife, Mrs. DuBois. Ladies, this is Lieutenant Rand Campbell. He has come to escort us into the fort."

"Call me Letty, dear," the older woman, a softer, plumper version of the daughter, murmured as she placed her round hand in Rand's.

Rand gripped it briefly and muttered some response, but his gaze was on the major's daughter. Her fiery red hair was arranged in a mass of curls that framed her delicate face in a halo of color. She smiled at him as though he were the first man she'd ever seen.

"I'm *very* pleased to meet you," she said softly. Her silky hand lingered on his.

Rand was aware he was staring, but he couldn't seem to stop. He told the private driving the ambulance to take Ranger and he would drive the ladies into the fort. All the while he was conscious of Jessica's blue eyes fastened on him. Sarah might not have wanted to be with him, but that didn't mean other women weren't interested.

Ben Croftner's wounds had healed from the beating he'd taken at Rand Campbell's hands, but his rage still simmered. He propped his boots on the gleaming surface of his new walnut coffee table and stared across the room at his brother.

"I saw Wade Montgomery at the feed store today, Labe."

Labe looked down at his hands. "That so?"

His brother's cautious tone told him that Labe still feared Rand. "Campbell is long gone. He won't stop my plans again."

"You need to give up that obsession with Sarah." Labe's hands twisted in his lap, and he didn't look at Ben, as if fearing his response.

As well he should. Ben gritted his teeth but didn't waste the time to chide him. "Wade is still in favor of a marriage between Sarah and me. He's going to do all in his power to make it happen."

"She won't have none of it. Not after what you did."

"She took my ring. I had rights."

Labe just ducked his head again. "Has he told Sarah?"

"No, but he's going to. His father isn't long for this world. Once he's gone, Sarah won't have anyone encouraging her in her crazy ideas. She'll be with me yet."

TWO

Sarah glanced out the kitchen window at the big elm tree, brilliant with October color. Wade would be home soon for dinner, and she wanted to get the meal over with so she could escape to her room and finish her book. Reading was the only thing that kept her thoughts from yearning for what she could never have. Her fingers went to the love token hanging from a chain around her neck.

A sound made her whirl around. "Papa, you startled me." She looked at him with new eyes, seeing his frailty and the yellow tinge of his skin.

He wheezed as he lowered himself into the chair she pulled out for him at the table. She sat beside him and began to peel potatoes.

Her father leaned back in his chair and sighed. "You should have gone with Rand, you know."

Sarah nicked her finger with the knife. "I couldn't leave you!"

"You're not a little girl anymore. And there comes a time in every person's life when he has to step out and stand on his own feet. Rand was ready, and I think you are too. We both know I won't be around much longer."

Her heart squeezed at the certainty in his eyes. "No, Papa."

He held up a hand at her protest. "You just don't want to admit it, my dear girl. I would rest easier if I knew you were settled and happy. I never expected you to give up without a fight. You had to fight to get him in the first place. Remember all the tears until I let you put your hair up and wear your mother's green satin dress for Christmas dinner with the Campbells the year you turned sixteen?"

Sarah smiled at the memory. "It worked too. That was the first time he saw me as anything but a pesky younger sister. But he's five states away now. What can I do?" Tears started into her eyes, and she brushed them away angrily.

Her father stood. "I don't know the answer, but I'm sure God will tell you if you'll listen." He patted the top of her head and turned to leave the kitchen.

She rose to run water over the potatoes and heard a sound behind her. A thump and a groan. Her heart in her throat, she whirled to see her father lying on the floor. Sarah flung herself down beside him and took his hand.

"Papa, it's me," she whispered. "Don't die, please don't die. Just hold on." She screamed Joel's name, then Rachel's.

At her voice, his pale lids fluttered and his cold fingers moved under hers. She leaned closer. "Don't try to talk. I'm here with you."

Her eight-year-old brother, Joel, came rushing down the steps. His face went ashen when he saw their father on the floor. "Get the doctor," she told him before bending back to Papa. Wade's wife, eight months pregnant, waddled into the hall from the parlor. She stopped and sank to her knees on the other side of Papa.

With an effort, Papa opened his eyes again and

tried to smile. "Don't cry, my dear girl. The Lord is waiting for me, and I'm going to be with your mama at last." He blinked a few times, then focused on her face. "Just be happy, Sarah. You fight for your Rand, if you must, and don't let Wade bully you into anything." He coughed weakly. "But don't leave Joel with Wade. Promise me." His voice grew stronger and he raised his head slightly. "Promise!"

"I promise," Sarah whispered as she felt his icy fingers loosen. The breath eased from his mouth. His chest didn't rise again. "Papa!" Sarah stared at him. This couldn't be real. He'd just been talking with her. She clutched his hand tighter. "Don't leave me, Papa!" She kissed his cheek and gathered his head into her lap. "Dear God, no," she sobbed. "Don't take him. This can't be happening." She looked over at Rachel kneeling and weeping on the other side of Papa's body. "He's just unconscious, Rachel. He can't be dead."

Rachel just shook her head and cried hard. "I'm so sorry, Sarah. We all loved him. He was a good man." She scooted around and put her arm around Sarah's shaking shoulders. "He never got over missing your mama. Just be happy he's finally with her again."

"But I still need him." Sarah's voice was bewildered as she stared down into her father's peaceful face. "He can't leave me now." She touched his grizzled cheek, already cooling.

They both turned as Wade and Doc Seth rushed in the door with Joel on their heels. "Help him, Doc," Sarah pleaded as the doctor knelt beside his friend of nearly forty years and put the stethoscope to her father's chest.

There was a long pause, then the doctor straightened. "I'm sorry, Sarah. William's gone." His voice was hoarse and moisture glistened in his eyes.

The words hammered into Sarah's brain. She reached for Joel, who had begun to cry. He was hers now. She had to keep her little brother safe and the family from splintering apart.

Amelia looked radiant as she turned to let Sarah button up her wedding dress. Sarah's heart filled at the joy on her face. At least there was some good in these dark days since her father's funeral. "You look beautiful. Jacob will be tongue-tied."

"I hope so." Amelia faced her. "I'm so glad you came. I wasn't sure you'd be up to it."

"I wouldn't miss it." Through the open window,

Sarah heard the sounds of buckboards and buggies as the guests began to arrive for the ceremony. "Papa said something before he died. He told me to fight for Rand. I can't do that from here. I want to go with you and Jacob when you leave for Fort Laramie."

Amelia's eyes went wide. "I would love that! I've been so fearful of being alone when Jacob is out on patrol. Having you there would make it all bearable."

Sarah's fingers went to the token at her neck. "Will Jacob agree?"

"I'm sure he will. I'll talk to him tonight." Amelia hugged her tight. "I can't tell you how pleased I am. Now let's go get me hitched." Her smile beamed out. "We're leaving in two days. Can you be ready by then?"

"Of course." Her thoughts raced as she tried to think of all she should bring. "What about Joel? I can't leave him behind. He belongs with me."

Amelia's smile seemed less certain, but she nodded. "You can't leave Wade to raise Joel."

As soon as the wedding was over, Sarah rushed home to pack. She had to tell Joel they were leaving too. She found him in the barn forking hay into the horse stalls. He paused to wipe his face, and she realized he was crying.

Dust motes danced in the air, and she sneezed at the hay. Joel dropped the pitchfork and rushed into her arms. She held him close, not minding that he smelled of horse manure and barn dirt. "We're going to be okay, Joel. Has Wade been hard on you?" Though he was still half boy, she was beginning to catch a glimpse of the man he would be with the right influences. Being away from Wade would be better for him.

He pulled away and shrugged. "Not any more than usual."

"I have something to tell you." She could barely keep her voice at a whisper. "We're leaving with Amelia and Jacob when they go to Fort Laramie."

His green eyes, so like her own, widened, and a smile lifted the corners of his lips. "For real?"

She nodded. "I need you to pack what you'll need in one suitcase. We'll have to travel as light as we can."

His smile faded. "Wade won't let us."

"He'll have no choice." She turned toward the barn door. "I'm going to fix dinner and then pack. Don't say anything until after I tell Wade."

She hurried into the kitchen and found Rachel at the table, cutting carrots. "Any labor pangs?"

Rachel shook her head. "Not yet." She rubbed her swollen belly. "I'm so ready."

The kitchen door banged open and Wade stomped in. "Supper's not done yet?" he growled as he hung up his red plaid jacket. He turned and looked at Sarah. "There's something I want to talk to you about."

She didn't trust his mild tone. He wanted something from her, and she had a sinking feeling she knew what it was. "What about?"

"Your future." He stared at her challengingly. "I saw Ben in town the other day, and for some reason he still wants to marry you. I told him I didn't see any reason why you wouldn't. That good-for-nothing Campbell went off and left you in the lurch and—"

"No." The short, clipped word cut him off just as he was picking up steam.

"You will do what I say. You're under age and my ward." Wade compressed his lips in an effort to keep his temper.

"I will *not* marry Ben. Rand and I belong together. Papa's last words to me were to fight for Rand. I'll never marry Ben."

"Well, that's just too bad, missy. You'd better get used to the idea because you will do as I say. Campbell has run off to the frontier, and you'll never see him again anyway." He shoved her toward the door. "You'll stay in your room until you agree to abide by my decisions." He grabbed her arm and dragged her up the stairs and into her room.

Sarah stared at the closed door in disbelief as the lock clicked shut behind her brother. His behavior had shocked her so much she hadn't put up much fight. "You can't keep me in here, Wade! This isn't the Middle Ages!" She heard him going down the steps and ran to the door. "Let me out of here. I'll never marry Ben—never!" She twisted the latch to no avail, then kicked at the solid oak door in a helpless frenzy of rage.

Pain exploded in her toe, and she hobbled over to sit on the bed and think. Joel would be in the house soon. He'd let her out. But what then? What could she do? She bit her lip and turned to look around her room. She could pack in peace.

Instead of asking to be let out, Sarah spent the night planning her escape and was bleary-eyed from lack of sleep by the time morning came. She and Joel had whispered through the door until they were both ready to go. She hid her suitcase under the bed just as she heard Wade's heavy tread outside the door.

The lock turned and he stepped into the room. She wanted to throw something at him as soon as she saw his smug face. "Ready to be reasonable yet?"

"Do I have a choice?" She kept her face averted so he couldn't see her eyes.

He smiled. "I knew you'd come around. I had Rachel save you some breakfast."

The exultation in his voice caused her to clench her hands to keep from screaming at him. "I'm not hungry."

He eyed her bent head, then seemed satisfied that he'd broken her spirit and nodded. "Fine. I'll go talk to Pastor Stevens, and we'll discuss when the wedding can take place." He left the door open behind him and tromped back downstairs and out the door.

Sarah sprang to her feet as soon as the buggy rumbled down the rutted track toward town. Feverishly she pulled her suitcase from under her bed. As she picked it up and turned toward the door, she heard someone in the hall. She froze until she realized it was just Joel.

His red hair didn't look as though it had been combed for days, but his eyes held more excitement than she'd seen in ages. "I've got my suitcase ready."

"Go get it, and I'll meet you downstairs."

"Can I take my rifle?"

Sarah hesitated as she looked into his pleading face. The less baggage the better, but the rifle had been Papa's and she didn't have the heart to make him leave it behind. She nodded, and he slung it over his shoulder and picked up his suitcase. They slipped down the steps and came face-to-face with Rachel.

She looked from the suitcases to Sarah's face. "You're leaving. I knew Wade would never force you to fall in with his plans—but who has ever been able to tell him anything?" She pushed her brown hair back from her forehead and held out her arms.

Sarah put down her suitcase and went to Rachel with a sigh. "I'll miss you, Rachel. But I have to find Rand." Her words were muffled against Rachel's shoulder. She drew away and looked into her sister-in-law's eyes. "Don't tell Wade I've gone."

Rachel smiled faintly. "He won't be back till suppertime. If you hurry, you can catch the afternoon train and be long gone before he knows you've left." She hugged her fiercely, then shoved her toward the door. "Write when you get there. And don't forget about me and the baby. We love you."

Sarah gulped and wiped her eyes. "I know, Rachel. And you've been a real sister to me. Make sure you write us when the baby's born."

Rachel nodded, then smiled through her tears and made a shooing motion with her apron. "You'd best get going. You have a lot to get done today."

Joel hurried ahead to hitch up the wagon while Sarah took one last look at the home where she'd been born. The sun shone through the bare trees in dappled patterns on the front porch roof. The solid two-story seemed so safe and familiar. She could see the red barn just behind it where she'd played in the haymow as a child. The chicken coop off to the east, the pasture beyond that, and all around the gently rolling hills of Montgomery land. It was all so heart-breakingly beloved.

She'd never had any plans of leaving her home. At least not any farther than the knoll beyond the pasture. Would she ever see it again? And who would tend Papa's grave?

She choked back tears and climbed up beside Joel. This was no time for tears, for second thoughts. Wade had left her no choice. She waved one last good-bye at Rachel, then stared firmly ahead.

THREE

S arah stared out the window of the stagecoach as the barren landscape swept by. The train portion of the trip had been much more pleasant. The stage-coach reeked of dusty leather, hair tonic, horse, and underlying everything else, the unlovely aroma of unwashed bodies. They'd lurched along for ten days already. Occasionally, several of the soldiers traveling with them tried to strike up a conversation, but they soon fell silent under Jacob's glowering.

The frozen landscape rolled past all that day and

through the night. The next morning was colder, and a hint of moisture was in the blustery wind. The soldiers predicted a blizzard but not until the next day. They should all be safe and snug in Fort Laramie by then.

Sarah sighed, and her breath steamed. "I hope I get a chance to bathe before I see Rand. I must look terrible." She could feel her hair hanging in straggly wisps against her cheeks. The last time she pushed it out of her face, her gloves had come away smeared with dirt. Rand would take one look at her and send her home.

Jacob shuffled his feet on the other side of Amelia as the driver gave a shout from topside. He grinned at Sarah. "Sounds like we're there."

Sarah moaned and tried to pat the strands of hair back into some semblance of order as she lifted the leather covering and peered out the window at the fort. Surrounded by rocky soil and sagebrush, it sprawled across the Laramie River, and its frame and adobe buildings lined a wide parade ground fortified with mountain howitzers. But it was all so barren. The fort seemed a tiny oasis in a vast plain of frigid wasteland.

She gave an involuntary gasp when she saw the Indians encamped all around the fort, their teepees gleaming in the sunshine. Hundreds of them. Women squatted around open fires, and children shouted and played in the dust.

"Has the fort been overrun? Is it safe to disembark?"

The garrulous old soldier across the aisle chuckled. "Fort Laramie's the headquarters for the Sioux. There's always a passel of Sioux 'round here. You'll git used to it." He nodded to her. "The name's Rooster, miss."

"But there's no stockade." She shuddered. "What if they turn hostile?"

"There's always plenty of hostiles around, but they know better than to attack a fort as well garrisoned as this one. You don't need to worry none, missy. The most them savages ever done was run howling through the pasture to stampede the horses."

Several soldiers manned a ferry, and the stagecoach rolled onto the vessel. Out on the river, the wind cut through Sarah's clothing. The soldiers guided the stagecoach horses off the ferry and onto the road, then stepped back. Sarah's heart pounded as the horses pulled the stage up the hill and it rolled to a stop. The driver threw open the door and helped the two ladies down before climbing on top and tossing the luggage down to the eager hands waiting below.

Sarah stared all around in dismay. It was not at

all as she'd imagined. The adobe buildings lining the parade ground looked cheerless and unwelcoming. A U.S. flag whipped forlornly in the wind atop a flag-pole on the far side of the parade ground. The fort seemed to be stuck out in the middle of nowhere with the wilderness all around. Most of the soldiers milling around stopped and stared at her and Amelia.

"It'll look better come spring," Rooster consoled.

Jacob piled their luggage together in a heap, then addressed a nearby soldier. "Could you tell me where we might find Lieutenant Rand Campbell?"

"Well don't this beat the Dutch." The soldier had a friendly, smiling face. "You've gotta be Jacob. You look enough like your brother to be two peas out of the same pod." The soldier stuck out a large calloused hand. "Isaac Liddle's my name, and Rand's my bunky."

Jacob shook his hand vigorously. "Mighty glad to meet you. Got any idea where that rascal brother of mine is?"

"Probably at mess. Bugle sounded a few minutes ago. I was headed there myself. Just follow me."

Shivering as much from nerves as from the cold, Sarah took Joel's hand and trailed behind Jacob and Amelia. She could hear shouts of laughter emanating from the officers' mess hall, and her stomach rumbled as the wind brought a mouthwatering aroma of stew to her nose.

She allowed herself a moment to imagine Rand's delight when he saw her. His dark brown eyes would light with love and surprise, and he'd rush to fold her in his arms. She could almost feel his heart thudding under her cheek now. It was all she could do not to break out in a smile.

The room was brightly lit with dozens of lanterns, and the general feeling of high spirits and fellowship warmed her as much as the heat rolling from the pot-bellied stove in the center of the room. She scanned the room quickly as their presence caused the babble of voices to soften, then still. She caught sight of Rand sitting at the far table next to two women. His handsome, square-jawed face was tanned and healthy.

Her first impulse was to call out his name and run to him, but the expression on his face as he gazed at the young redheaded woman stopped her. Sarah didn't like the dazed smile on his face or the possessive hand the woman had on his arm.

She gulped as he looked up and saw them. "Rand." She managed a tremulous smile.

He rose to his feet as the small party neared. "I didn't expect you for at least another week or two." He grabbed his brother's hand and pumped it, then hugged Amelia and Joel but didn't touch Sarah. "Hello, Sarah, Joel."

"Who are all these folks, Rand?" The woman stood and slid her hand into the crook of Rand's arm. Her perfume, some exotic flowery scent, mingled with the scent of stew. "Introduce me to your friends."

He hesitated and didn't meet Sarah's gaze. "Jessica, this is my brother Jacob; his wife, Amelia; a-and some friends from back home, Sarah Montgomery and her brother Joel."

"Pleased to meet you all." She turned a bright smile toward Jacob. "I've heard all about you, Jacob. Rand tells me you're the county boxing champion." Her smile deepened into a dimple. "I'm Jessica DuBois, and this is my mother, Mrs. Major DuBois."

The address sounded strange to Sarah, but that was how wives were addressed in the army. Jessica had aqua eyes and deep red hair that shimmered in the candlelight. Her skin was almost translucent, with a pale peach tint to her high cheekbones and full lips. Jessica's mother was a blurred image of her daughter with softer, plumper lines and a gentle expression.

"Please call me Letty, dear. Everyone does." She smiled at Amelia and Sarah. "I'm so glad to have two other women here at Laramie. We must get together for tea tomorrow. We ladies have to stick together. It helps the time go by. And you all are here just in time to help plan the wedding."

"Wedding?" Sarah looked at Rand. "Whose wedding?"

"Why, mine and Rand's, of course." Jessica hit Rand on the arm with her fan. "Why, you bad boy, haven't you told your family about us yet?"

"They had probably left Wabash by the time my letter got there," Rand said, his eyes on Sarah's face.

Sarah felt as though she were falling. She couldn't catch her breath. How could he? How could he come out and get engaged in less than two months? She fought down the tight tears in her throat as she gripped Amelia's hand. She didn't want to give the other woman the satisfaction of seeing her cry. Did she know Sarah had once been engaged to Rand?

"Congratulations," Jacob said after an awkward pause. "I had no idea you were seeing anyone."

"Rand, our journey has been long. I think we all need a place to rest and recover," Sarah said through tight lips. "Could you see about finding us a place to stay tonight?"

She just wanted to find a private corner where she could come to grips with this new reality—so very different from what she'd expected. Her face felt stiff, and if she relaxed her guard she'd fall apart.

"The quartermaster is by the door. Come with me, Jacob, and we'll get you all fixed up."

Joel tugged on Sarah's arm. "How can Rand marry that lady when he's going to marry you?"

Jessica choked on her coffee. "Why, whatever does the boy mean?"

Sarah's face burned and she wanted to run away, but she lifted her chin, determined to preserve her dignity if she could. "Rand and I were engaged before the war. Rand and I have been friends all our lives."

Jessica bit her lip and looked at her mother. "I see."

Sarah forced a smile. "If Rand is happy, I'm happy. I want to be friends with you too." She could sense Amelia's silent approval of her soft answer.

"Well, um, that's fine then," Jessica finally muttered as Jacob hurried back over to them.

"We're all fixed up," Jacob announced. "Let's go get settled. Rand will bring us over some stew after we get cleaned up."

Sarah felt numb as she held on to her skirts and

followed the little party across the windy parade ground. How could all her hopes and dreams end like this? What could she do?

Rand led them to an adobe building. "Captain Leeks lives on the other side with his family, but his family never stays here in the winter. His wife and two sons will be back in May."

He opened the door and led them into a narrow hall that opened onto a small, cheerless parlor. The room was cold and barren with plain plank floors. It smelled musty from disuse but had a lingering odor of smoke and soot. Sarah glanced around. At least they wouldn't sleep on the ground tonight, and they were out of the wind.

Rand knelt at the fireplace and poked at the logs. "I'll have it warmed up in no time." He got the fire going, then stood. "I'll leave you to get cleaned up. I'll be back in about an hour with some supper for you." He grinned. "Cooky likes me. When he hears we have two new ladies, he'll be glad to whip up something."

"You're hardly limping at all now," Jacob said.

"Horse riding and walking has strengthened my leg a lot." He turned toward the door.

When he started toward the door, Sarah stepped into his path. She laid her hand on his arm, and the muscles in his forearm flexed under her fingers. "We need to talk."

Rand stared down at her and swallowed. "I'll be back later. We'll talk then."

"Now, please."

Rand sighed and ran his hand through his hair. "Sarah, you need to unpack and get settled in. And we need to talk in private."

He was right. What was there to explain? It was pretty self-explanatory. No wonder he wasn't eager to discuss it with her. Was this the same man she'd known all her life? She stepped out of his way and watched him pull the door shut behind him.

Amelia touched her shoulder. "Are you all right?"

Sarah's eyes burned, but she refused to let the tears fall. She had to be strong for Joel's sake. He'd been through too much, and she couldn't let him sense her despair.

She swallowed. "I'll be all right. I just need a bit of time to adjust."

In the tiny kitchen there was a Sibley stove that Jacob soon had blazing. The warmth crept into the room and seeped into Sarah's cold skin, but nothing could reach her icy heart. A battered kettle sat on the stove. She rinsed it with water from the bucket a private brought to the back door. First they'd have a cup of tea and then see to bathing the road dust off their sore bodies. She felt as though the fine yellow grit was in every pore of her body. She could even taste its gritty presence. She looked around the small quarters. Only one bedroom opened off the kitchen. Where could they all sleep?

"I'll bring over a couple more bunks," Jacob said. "We can put one in the parlor and use it for a sofa during the day. You can sleep there, Sarah. I'll put another one in the entry for Joel, and everyone will have a little privacy. Just for tonight, you and Amelia can sleep in the bedroom, and Joel and I will put up in the barracks." He hauled the hip bath down off its peg on the wall and set it in the small bedroom. He stuck his head out the door and asked a private to go down to the river and haul some water for bathing.

Even with several kettles of boiling water added, the bathwater was barely tepid, so Sarah bathed quickly. She was ravenous by the time Rand brought over a steaming kettle of stew and bread. They wolfed down their supper in ten minutes.

Jacob yawned. "I'm beat. I think the rest of us will

turn in. Good night, honey." He kissed Amelia, then gestured for Joel to join them. The door lock snicked shut behind them.

Amelia stood. "Good night. Don't be too late, Sarah. I know you're exhausted." She sent a stern glance Rand's way before stepping to the bedroom and closing the door.

The silence stretched between them. Sarah pleated the folds of her skirt and couldn't look at Rand.

He rose and paced to the window. "I never thought I'd see you again."

"So it appears." She forced the words out of her tight throat. "I came out to keep Amelia company." She couldn't bear for him to know she'd come here expecting a much different reception. "I didn't expect to find you engaged so quickly though."

Rand raked a hand through his brown hair and his lips flattened. "I know it looks bad, Sarah, but I had a lot of time to think these past few months. I like army life. The adventure, the sense of doing something worthwhile. Something that affects other people besides just my family. I want to be part of taming the West for my country."

Sarah stared up at him. "What about your family

back in Wabash? You sound as if you never intend to go home." Though he'd said as much back in Wabash, she'd been sure he hadn't meant it, not really.

"Tell me honestly, does the thought of living in the wilderness appeal to you? You were quick to let me go alone." He knelt beside her chair. "Please try to understand."

She inhaled his manly scent mixed with the pungent odor of wood smoke, then reached out and touched his cheek, rough with stubble under her fingers. Heat flared between them before he rocked back on his heels and stood. "All I want is for you to be happy."

Hurt flashed in his eyes. "I never dreamed you'd follow me, Sarah," he said hoarsely. "If I'd even suspected it . . ." His voice trailed off. "I've made a commitment to Jessica now. She'll make an excellent army wife. She's lived in frontier forts most of her life. It hurt when you didn't love me enough to leave your family for me. Jessica will go wherever I'm sent without a complaint. She understands soldiers and their duties."

Rand turned his back to her and paced to the window. A bugle sounded in the distance. "She was here when I was hurting over your rejection. She let me know right off how she felt." He wheeled around to face her again. "What are you doing here, anyway? You said you wouldn't leave your father."

"Papa's dead." She touched his arm as she saw the hurt and shock register on his face, feelings that mirrored her own. "His heart just . . . gave out."

"Oh, Sarah." He ran a hand through his thick hair. "I really loved your pa. He was like a father to me."

"He loved you too," she said softly. "He spoke of you just before he died."

"He did?"

She nodded. "He was gone just a few minutes after we'd talked. He told me—" She broke off and bit her lip.

"He told you what?"

"It's not important now. But I didn't want Amelia to be alone."

Rand's mouth tightened. "Is that why you're here? Now that your father is gone and you don't have anything else to do, you came out here? It had nothing to do with me?"

Sarah looked down. "Do you love Jessica?" Her face felt so stiff she could barely move her lips. She had to know the answer, but her heart pounded.

"Not like I loved you. But she's been good to me.

She's very sweet and kind. I can't just throw her off like a busted saddle. I gave her my word."

Sarah stared at him. "We said good-bye before you left. Nothing has really changed." Tears burning her eyes, she stood and opened the door.

FOUR

"What do you mean she's gone?" Ben kicked at Wade's hound that had come nosing from under the porch of the Montgomery house. "Where is she?"

The wind lifted Wade's hair. "Off to find Campbell, I would guess. I checked at the train station, and she and Joel left with Jacob and Amelia." He opened the door. "Let's get out of the wind."

Ben followed him into the parlor where a crackling fire radiated warmth into the room. He held his hands at the blaze before turning to face Wade. "You let this happen. You said she'd do what you told her."

Wade dropped onto the horsehair sofa. "This is not my fault. You were the one who lied to her. She puts a lot of stock in honesty."

A thin cry echoed from upstairs. "That your kid?"

Wade nodded. "A boy. Sarah never even stayed to make sure Rachel delivered. I'm washing my hands of her. She can have whatever wretched life she wants with Campbell."

Ben could imagine the tender scene, and hatred soured his belly. "He won't keep her. A woman like Sarah needs a firm hand."

"She's always been besotted with him. I should have known it was a losing battle."

"I never lose." Ben shoved his hands in his pockets. "I'm going after her."

A plan began to form. He had connections in Washington, and while he'd never thought to go West, there were many opportunities for a clever man to become rich off the Indian Wars.

Rand was already awake when reveille sounded at five. Jacob and Joel were sleepily pulling on their overalls and boots when he strode into the bunk room to check on them. "Hurry up or you'll miss the cold slop we call breakfast."

"How's the Indian situation?" Jacob poured icy water out of a battered tin pitcher into a chipped bowl and splashed his eyes, bleary from lack of sleep.

A group of soldiers had been up playing cards all night, and their loud talk and laughter had made sleep difficult, especially with Sarah's words still running through Rand's head. Most of them had already cleared out of the long room lined with bunks, but the odor of hair tonic and dirty socks still lingered.

Rand handed his brother the cleanest towel he could find. "Bad. And likely to get worse. The Bureau of Indian Affairs has really botched things. Every agent they've sent sets out to line his pockets with what belongs to the Indians. Once one gets rich enough, he goes back east and another comes to start the same process all over again." Rand shook his head. "And it's really explosive up in the Powder River area. Quite a few miners have been killed trying to get to the gold fields."

"Much hostility around here?"

"Not really. A few skirmishes. There's mostly tame Oglala Sioux and friendly Brulé. Most of the wild Oglala are with Red Cloud at Powder River."

"The girls will be relieved to hear that."

"I was just about to check on them." Rand paused.

The smell of impending snow freshened the air and the wind stung their cheeks as they hurried across the parade ground toward the light spilling out the front window of the house. It looked warm and welcoming in the somber darkness of the predawn morning. Their breath made frosty plumes in the air, and their boots crunched against the frozen ground as they waved and called morning greetings to the soldiers heading toward the mess hall, most of them shrouded in buffalo robes against the cold. The trumpet's call to breakfast carried clearly in the clear air.

Sarah's heart was heavy as she dropped her dress over her bustle. The pagoda sleeves were quite fashionable, and at least she could hold her head up in Jessica's presence. She added a tatted collar and her favorite brooch, a rose filigree Rand had given her, then took her hairpins and went to find Amelia in the kitchen.

Rand and Jacob should be here anytime, and she wanted a moment with him. She wasn't sure what she should do. She couldn't go back home. The journey had been so arduous, she couldn't bear to think of making it again. And besides, she refused to be under Wade's thumb again. Having been his virtual prisoner had soured her against him.

She turned as she heard the men thump up the porch steps and ran to unlock the door. "Good morning." Her gaze went to Rand.

He didn't look at her. "Breakfast will be over if you two don't hurry up."

"We're almost ready. Let me finish my hair. Jacob, why don't you take Amelia and Joel and go on ahead?" Sarah's words were mumbled through a mouthful of hairpins, and she began to wind her braids up at the base of her head. With an understanding glance, Amelia adjusted her bonnet, then drew on her navy cape and followed Jacob and Joel out the door.

Sarah finished her hair with a few quick thrusts of well-placed hairpins, then looked up at Rand. "Is my being here going to be a problem for you?"

He looked away and swallowed hard. "Of course not. We'll always be friends."

She'd thought they were so much more. "I don't want to cause you any trouble."

He shrugged. "You can stay here with Jacob and Amelia. And if you want one, you won't have any trouble finding a beau. It's so rare for the men to see any unattached women—you'll probably have a dozen proposals before the week is over."

Stung by his words, Sarah tossed her head back. "I don't give my affections as easily as some."

Hurt flashed in his eyes before his expression grew guarded. "Jacob said he'd probably be sent to one of the northern forts come late spring or early summer, so I reckon we can be civil to one another for a few months."

He picked up her cloak from the foot of the bed and held it out to her courteously. She let its warmth enfold her before swishing away from him without another word. The wind struck her as she stepped onto the porch, and as she staggered, Rand caught her arm and steadied her. She was very conscious of his strong, warm fingers pressing against her arm through her cape.

His brown eyes were impersonal as he gazed down

on her. "The wind is ferocious out here. Watch your step." He led her across the parade ground toward the mess hall, the soft glow of lamplight shining out its windows and a lazy curl of smoke rising from its chimney.

With an effort, Sarah controlled her hurt and anger. She forced a smile and laid a hand on his arm before stepping into the mess hall.

It was a big open room filled with long wooden tables that seated eight to ten men. The tables closest to the stove in the center of the room were all filled.

"Rand!" Jessica, clad in a green dress, was seated across the table from Jacob, Amelia, and Joel at the table closest to the stove. She waved to them.

The other woman's shining red hair was elegantly piled high on her head, and her pale complexion was flawless. Her mother had the same cool loveliness. Sarah wanted to like her, wanted to believe Rand had made a good choice.

She smiled at her. "Good morning, Miss DuBois. You look lovely this morning. I like your dress."

Jessica smiled and the hostility in her eyes faded. "I hope you rested well, Miss Montgomery."

"I did, yes. And please, call me Sarah."

Jessica nodded, then looked up to Rand. "Don't

forget the new play at Bedlam is tonight. You did say you'd pick me up at seven, right?"

Rand nodded, and Sarah clenched her fists in the folds of her skirt until she could breathe past the pain.

"You must come, Miss Montgomery. You and your friends." Mrs. DuBois fluttered her plump, white hands. "My husband has the lead role, and you'll be able to meet all the officers."

"Please call me Sarah," she said automatically, her gaze on Rand and Jessica.

"It will be so pleasant to have other ladies at the fort." Letty shuddered delicately. "One gets so lonesome for the refined company of other women in this primitive place. Perhaps we can get together for tea tomorrow?"

Sarah forced herself to smile and accept Letty's invitation as she strained to listen to Jessica's monopoly of Rand's conversation. Obviously, he had spent considerable time with this woman and enjoyed her company. Did Rand really love her? Sarah swallowed hard. She'd accept whatever she had to.

The breakfast lasted an interminable amount of time as they ate the nearly cold flapjacks and grits and washed it all down with strong, hot coffee. Nearly every officer in the place found some excuse to stop at their table for an introduction. Jacob glowered at the attention Amelia received, but Rand just looked on impassively as the younger officers flirted with Sarah and paid her extravagant compliments.

After breakfast the quartermaster gave them rough woolen blankets, a couple of crude wooden beds with straw mattresses, and a water bucket. Amelia had brought a trunk packed with kitchen utensils and plates as well as some bright calico and gingham material, several sets of muslin sheets, and some quilts she'd made over the years.

"You're so well prepared," Sarah said. "Look at my meager belongings. I have to throw myself on your mercy."

Amelia smiled. "I've been preparing for this for a year. Anything I own is yours, and you know it."

As they carried their booty back to their quarters, Sarah was able to take a good look at their new home. Darkness had fallen so quickly last night, she hadn't really noticed much about it. A front porch ran the width of the house with wide front steps. Two doors opened off the unpainted porch.

Rand opened the main door, and they stepped inside the wide, bare entry hall. The first door led to the tiny sitting room that looked out on the front porch.

COLLEEN COBLE

Sarah stood gazing around with her hands on her hips. There were definite possibilities. She walked through the narrow door in the small kitchen and surveyed the Sibley stove in the middle of the tiny room. There was just enough space in the corner for a small table. Hooks could be hung from the low roof for pots, and a small corner cupboard could be built in the adjoining parlor.

She turned to catch an expression of dismay on her friend's face. "What do you think, Amelia?"

Amelia brushed a stray wisp of dark hair out of her eyes. "I don't know where to begin. You take charge, Sarah. You're so much better at decisions than I am."

By midafternoon the tiny rooms had been scrubbed, Jacob had tacked the wool blankets to the floor in the sitting room and bedroom, fires blazed in all three fireplaces, and the beds were set up and ready for occupancy. Sarah and Amelia each had a lapful of material as they stitched curtains for the windows and cloths to cover the crates that would suffice as tables. Sarah could hear the thunk of axes behind the house where Joel and Jacob were chopping more wood. Isaac had told them to let the wood detail bring them more logs, but Jacob insisted he needed the exercise after the cramped stagecoach journey.

She glanced around the room in satisfaction as she sewed. They could write and ask Rachel to send a rug for the sitting room. With a few trinkets and pictures, it would be quite homey. At least it was beginning to feel like home.

FIVE

The bustling of the fort awakening for a new day surrounded the small quarters. Sarah yawned and slipped out of bed to peek out the window, wincing as her feet hit the icy floor. The sun glowed as it began to peek out of the eastern hills. The wind still whistled through the eaves, but the snow had stopped.

Her sense of anticipation faded when she remembered today's plans. She and Amelia had promised Mrs. DuBois they'd come to lunch at eleven. The last thing she wanted was to hear details about the wedding. And Jessica was cruel enough to delight in seeing if she could make Sarah squirm. She pressed her lips together and turned to survey her wardrobe. She'd be cool and calm. No matter what Jessica said or how much it hurt, she wouldn't let her see her pain.

By the time Amelia and Jacob opened their bedroom door, Sarah had already gone through her trunk and decided on a dress. It was a deep-green poplin trimmed with black velvet and edged with lace. A sleeveless jacket of black corded silk went over the dress and cinched over her tiny waist. Her father had bought it for her from an elegant shop in Indianapolis just six months before he died. An intricate design of velvet ribbon adorned the skirt and sleeves. Sarah had always loved the dress.

"Good morning," she called to Amelia and Jacob. She tested the curling tongs on the kitchen stove with a wet finger. It sizzled. Good. Almost hot enough.

"You're up early." Amelia yawned. "What's the occasion?"

"Have you forgotten we have a date for lunch?"

Amelia eyed her uncertainly. "You seem almost pleased. I thought you were dreading it." She put a skillet on the stove and turned to mix up a batch of biscuits.

"Don't bother with breakfast for me," Jacob interrupted. "I'm running late. I'll grab something at officers' mess." He kissed Amelia and grabbed his coat off the hook by the stove.

"Be careful," Amelia called before turning her attention back to Sarah.

"I was really hating the thought of having to be nice to Jessica, but then I decided it would just be a challenge. There must be some good in her or Rand wouldn't care about her."

Amelia smiled. "I wish you luck finding it. I haven't seen it yet."

"My, that doesn't sound like you. I've never known you to have a bad word to say about anyone but Ben. You're always telling me to have more patience with people."

Amelia's cheeks flooded with pink. "I know I shouldn't feel that way, but she makes me uneasy just as Ben did."

"Well, she's not married to Rand yet. Papa told me to fight for him." She swallowed at the thought of her father. "Could you help me with my hair? I want to look my best."

Amelia nodded and the girls spent the next hour

curling Sarah's glistening red-gold locks. They pulled her heavy hair back from her face and let the back cascade down in tight curls. After pulling a few curls forward by her ears, Sarah was finally satisfied.

Amelia looked pretty and demure in a deep blue silk dress with a lace collar and lace around the sleeves. Her dark hair was pulled back in a loose knot at the nape of her neck with a few loose curls escaping at the sides.

Sarah threw her best cloak of brown wool with bands of velvet fringe over her shoulder, tied on her green silk bonnet, and walked toward the door with Amelia in tow. Knowing she looked her best helped calm her agitation.

But when Mrs. DuBois opened the door and Sarah saw Jessica standing behind her, she felt dowdy and plain. Jessica wore a lilac-colored silk dress with an intricate pattern in the skirt. Rows of lace ruffles cascaded over the skirt and sleeves, and her lovely white shoulders were bare. Her hair was braided and looped in an intricate way Sarah had never seen. The style accentuated Jessica's high cheekbones and big blue eyes.

But Mrs. DuBois was easy to like in spite of her daughter. "Come in, come in, my dears." She fluttered her plump hands as she drew them inside the warm hallway. "We've been so looking forward to this, haven't we, Jessica dear?"

"I certainly have."

Sarah thought she detected the hint of a sneer in Jessica's smooth voice. Sarah squared her shoulders as she handed her cloak and bonnet to Mrs. DuBois.

Jessica led the way into their cheerily decorated quarters. Since Major DuBois was a senior officer, he received more deluxe accommodations than a lowly lieutenant. The parlor was large with a soft flowered carpet on the wood floor. Dainty tables and a horse-hair sofa and three chairs furnished the room. Garden pictures and gold sconces adorned two walls while the fireplace dominated the third. Sarah could see the dining room through the arched doorway. A fine walnut table and chairs on another beautiful carpet occupied the center of the room. A young, attractive black woman hovered near the table.

"Rose, please pour our guests some tea," Mrs. DuBois called. "Sit down, ladies, please. I've been so looking forward to getting to know one another a little better."

Sarah sat on the sofa, expecting Amelia to sit next to her, but Jessica quickly settled there. With a glance at Sarah, Amelia sat on one of the chairs while Mrs. DuBois took possession of another one.

"What do you think of Fort Laramie so far? Are you ready to return to Indiana?" Mrs. DuBois asked.

"It's much more primitive than I expected," Sarah admitted. "And so cold. It seems very isolated."

"It's really very jolly in the summer. More ladies are here, and we have dances and parties almost every night. Wait until then before you decide to leave us."

"They'll be gone by then, Mother. Won't you?" Jessica addressed her last remark to Sarah.

Sarah forced herself to smile. "Who really knows with the army? We're hoping to stay near Rand as long as we can." She heard Jessica's sharp intake of breath.

"Excuse me for a moment, ladies," Mrs. DuBois said, seemingly unaware of the awkward pause. "I just want to peek in to see how our lunch is coming." She scurried away and disappeared behind the door on the far side of the dining room.

As soon as her mother was gone, Jessica glared at Sarah. "Just what did you mean by that remark? I've already warned you not to meddle. Nothing is going to stop this wedding. You try and I promise you, you'll be very, very sorry."

"I didn't mean anything other than we all love Rand and want to be with him as long as we can. He was gone three years and only home a few days before coming out here." Sarah looked into Jessica's eyes. "I won't lie to you and tell you I don't still love him. But I want him to be happy, and if that means marriage to you, I'll try to accept that."

Jessica's face whitened as her mother came back into the room. The look she cast at Sarah was full of venom, and Sarah could see the effort it took for her to control herself in her mother's presence.

The next hour was spent in light conversation over a delicious tea of dainty chicken salad sandwiches, tiny cakes, and cookies. The entire time Jessica's anger seethed just under her smooth surface.

"Do come again," Mrs. DuBois urged as she handed them their cloaks and bonnets. "I so enjoyed your company."

After promising they would come again, Amelia and Sarah made their escape. Amelia let out a sigh as soon as the door closed and they stepped down onto the path back home. "You've made a real enemy, Sarah. Jessica seems capable of anything."

Sarah sighed. "I meant to try to be on friendly

terms with her. I really want Rand to be happy." Tears sparkled on her lashes. "Watching him marry Jessica will be the hardest thing I've ever done, though."

They reached their door and Joel came tearing out.

Sarah caught him as he tried to rush past them. "Whoa. What's going on?" Before Joel could answer, Rand strolled out behind him.

"We're going ice fishing," Rand said. "With your permission, of course. I was going to ask before I took him, but I wasn't sure where you were, and he assured me you wouldn't mind."

"No, of course I don't mind. And we were at the DuBois's for tea," she added as he turned to go.

He stopped and gave her a quick look. "I see," was all he said. He cleared his throat. "Well, we'll be going now. He'll be back in time for supper."

"Have fun." Her heart ached as she watched him match his stride to Joel's shorter one. Her brother looked up at him adoringly as they walked away. Would things ever be right? Was it even possible to untangle this mess? She sighed and followed Amelia into the house.

Rand rapped at Colonel Maynadier's door.

"Enter."

He stepped inside the room, taking in the piles of papers scattered over the old wooden desk before saluting smartly. "You wanted to see me, sir?"

"Ah yes, Lieutenant Campbell." The colonel looked up from his scrutiny of the document in front of him. He was a tall, spare man somewhere in his forties with blond, thinning hair and pale eyebrows. But there was nothing nondescript about his eyes. They were gray and eagle sharp. The soldiers under his command knew those eyes missed nothing that concerned the well-being of Fort Laramie. Rand sometimes thought the colonel could see inside his soul with those eyes. "Camp rumor has it that a certain Lieutenant Jacob Campbell is your brother and that he arrived a few days ago with a wife and her companion. Is that correct?"

"Yes, sir."

"Excellent. I have a proposition for you. Big Ribs and some of the other chiefs have asked for their children to be instructed in the basics of a white education. Learning English, a little reading and writing. I would like to request that Miss—" He peered at the paper in front of him. "That Miss Montgomery take over the task while she is here. Lieutenant Liddle informs me that she is a most gifted, intelligent young woman and not likely to be frightened by the Indian children."

Rand swallowed his dismay. "I'll ask her, sir." The last thing he wanted was to get Sarah even more entangled in life at Fort Laramie.

He kept his face impassive as the colonel outlined his plan for the school. He'd had a hard time keeping his emotions under control the last few evenings as the five of them had curled up on the floor beside the fireplace and played checkers after he and Joel had returned from their fishing expedition. She laughed and teased like the Sarah he'd loved so long and so well. The last few evenings had been pure torture. How long must he endure her presence? He'd decided to turn his life in a new direction, and he would stick with it.

"One other thing," Colonel Maynadier said as Rand saluted and turned to go. "There's a new authorized fur trader to the Sioux downriver. Please check in on him this afternoon and see that he understands the rules governing Indian trade."

"Yes, sir." Another fur trader was the least of his worries, he fumed as he strode across the snow-covered parade ground. They were all alike anyway. All set on feathering their own nests at the expense of the Indians. They forced the Indians to pay for their own annuities with furs and made exorbitant profits when they sold the furs back east.

Sarah opened the door at his knock. Amelia was dressing in the bedroom and Jacob had already left for his duties.

Sarah's eyes darkened when he repeated the colonel's request. "When does he want me to start?"

"Right away. You're to use the chapel for now, and next spring the colonel plans to build a small schoolhouse. You'll have to improvise, though. There are no schoolbooks here and probably won't be for months." He stared at her downcast gaze. "You don't want to do it?"

She looked up then. "I'd like to help out, but I've never taught before. Teaching children who don't even know English very well sounds very difficult."

"Some of the teenagers will speak pretty well, and they'll help you with the younger ones."

She didn't look convinced. "I can try if you want me to."

"Can I go too?" Joel asked.

Sarah's brows winged up. "You actually *want* to learn something?"

Joel looked down at the floor. "There aren't any other boys to play with. I thought maybe I could teach some of them how to play baseball."

Sarah's face softened and she nodded. "We need to get on with your studies too." She turned back to Rand. "Could you find me some slate? Or some paper to lay across boards?"

"There's plenty of slate in the cliffs across the river. I'll fetch some this afternoon. I have to go that direction anyway to check on a new fur trader."

Was that tenderness in his face? It was probably just wishful thinking.

SIX

The sun shone coldly on the glistening snow as Rand threaded his way through the massive snowdrifts along the rocky trail that led downriver to the trader's establishment. He was cold through and through by the time he reached the group of small buildings bustling with activity. The pure snow had been tramped to a muddy quagmire by the horses tied to posts along the front of the buildings. They stood with their heads down and their backsides to the cutting gale.

Sioux and Cheyenne women huddled out of the

wind in the doorway of the storage building. He caught a glimpse of crates piled nearly to the ceiling through the open doorway. Trying to ignore the stench of so many unwashed bodies, he pushed his way into the smoke-filled room and looked around for someone in charge.

A scrawny, red-necked young man with stringy blond hair seemed to be directing the dispersal of crates. Impatience was etched around his mouth as he argued with a young Sioux brave. "We ain't giving out no ammunition. You can have some extra bean rations."

"Beans, bah! Must have gunpowder!" The Sioux warrior spat for emphasis at the young man's feet.

"Learn to grow crops like normal folk, and you wouldn't have to worry about shootin' buffalo. Now either take your rations and go, or get out of the way so the rest can get their grub."

The young brave scowled and swept the rations into the skirt the woman with him held ready. He gave the young man one last glare before stomping away.

Rand pushed his way up to the counter, and the man looked up. "Lieutenant Rand Campbell. I was ordered to see if there's anything you need. You are the new trader, aren't you?"

The young man licked his lips, and his eyes darted toward a door to the side of the counter. "No, sir. Name's Les Johnson and I just work for him. He's in his office right now with some folks. I'll tell him you stopped by, though."

"You do that. I have another errand to run. I'll stop back later this afternoon." Rand turned to leave and almost ran into a familiar lanky figure with dirty blond hair and pale blue eyes. "Labe?" Rand stared, almost not believing his own eyes, but it was definitely Labe Croftner. What was he doing here? His blood pounded in his ears, and he swallowed the lump of rage in his throat. "Where's Ben?" Labe would never roam this far from home without his brother.

"R-Rand!" Labe's eyes widened and he started to back away, but Rand grabbed his arm so tightly he flinched.

"Where is he?"

His face white, Labe shook his head, but his eyes darted to the closed door to the right of the counter. Rand released his arm and strode toward the door.

"Wait, you can't go in there!" Labe moved to intercept him, but Rand brushed by him and threw open the door.

Ben was seated at a makeshift desk with two rough-looking men dressed in buckskin sitting across from him on crates. His gray eyes widened when he saw Rand, then he smiled and stood, swiping his white-blond hair out of his face. "Well, well, well, if it isn't the illustrious Lieutenant Campbell come to pay me a call. I didn't expect word of my arrival to reach you quite this soon."

"What are you doing here, Croftner?" Rand clenched his fists and took a step toward the desk.

"What does it look like? I'm the new trader, old friend. This opportunity was too good to pass up, so I decided to put up with the disagreeable thought of having to run into you occasionally and took the job." Ben offered Rand an insolent smile and sat back down. "And a very lucrative one, too, I might add. Now if you don't mind, I have business to attend to."

Rand choked back his rage. He needed a clear head to deal with Croftner. There was some nefarious purpose to Ben's presence here, he was sure. "I'll be watching you, Croftner. You step out of line just one inch, and I'll be all over you like a wolf on a rabbit."

Ben smiled indolently. "I'm terrified. Can't you see me shake?" The other men guffawed, and he leaned forward. "Give Sarah my love, and tell her I'll stop and see her real soon."

Rand gritted his teeth. "You stay away from Sarah."

"My, my. Does your lovely fiancée know how you still feel about Sarah? Perhaps I should inform her how you're still looking after the poor little orphan." He sat back and crossed his muddy boot over his knee. "But the beautiful Jessica doesn't have anything to worry about. Sarah belongs to me, and she's going to discover that real soon."

"You lay one finger on Sarah, and you'll be in the guardhouse so fast you won't know what happened."

"Hey, there's no law against calling on a lady."

"She doesn't want to see you."

"I think I'll just let her tell me that. I'm sure she'd be pretty cut up about discovering her precious Rand is about to marry someone else."

Tired of the exchange, Rand clenched his jaw. This was getting him nowhere. He turned and stalked out the door as the men behind him burst into raucous laughter.

His jaw tight and his chest pounding, Rand swung up into the saddle. Ranger danced a bit, as if to ask what the trouble was. Rand patted his neck, then urged him down the trail back to the fort. Did Sarah know Ben would follow her out here? How much did she really care for Croftner? After all, she had agreed to marry him once.

When he arrived back at the fort, he marched over to see Sarah. She had her sleeves rolled up, and tendrils of hair had escaped her neat roll. A smudge of flour marred her flushed cheek, and she moved the loaf of rising dough out of the way.

He resisted the urge to reach out and wipe it off. "I got your slate."

She smiled and rubbed at the smudge of flour on her face. "Thanks for tending to it so quickly. I'm a little scared about it, Rand. What if I can't teach them? I don't know any Sioux words at all."

"You'll do fine, Sarah." He stuffed his hands in his pockets. "Heard from Ben lately?"

A frown crouched between her eyes. "No, and I don't expect to. I made my feelings about him very clear."

The tightness eased from his chest. "He's here, Sarah."

Her eyes widened. "Here? As in Fort Laramie?"

He nodded. "He's the new fur trader. He's crooked enough to make a good one."

She eyed him. "You've talked to him?"

"I think he came because you're here. He said to give you his love."

Her scarlet cheeks went white. "He was just trying to annoy you. He knows I never want to see him again."

Ben was just as full of lies as he'd always been. Rand resolved to alert the soldiers to keep an eye on Sarah and make sure Croftner didn't pull anything.

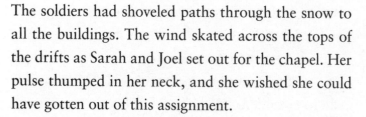

The soldiers had shoveled paths through the snow to all the buildings. The wind skated across the tops of the drifts as Sarah and Joel set out for the chapel. Her pulse thumped in her neck, and she wished she could have gotten out of this assignment.

Joel carried the stacks of slate for her. She didn't want him to grow up uneducated, and he was curious about the Indian children. It was a good way to interest him in studies. As she approached the small chapel, a group of about thirty youngsters watched her advance. She noticed one older girl of about seventeen. She was truly beautiful, with soft, dark eyes, glossy black braids, and an eager look on her face.

The girl stepped forward as Sarah stopped in front of the door. "I am Morning Song, daughter of White Raven," she said softly. "I very glad to learn more English."

The yearning in the young woman's face touched Sarah. "You speak well already." She opened the door and led them inside. Someone had already started a fire in the stove, and the room was warm and welcoming. She motioned for the children to be seated and waited until the rustling stopped.

"I'm Miss Sarah." She didn't want them to have to start off with a difficult word like Montgomery. "Can you say Miss Sarah?"

Dark eyes stared at her solemnly, then Morning Song spoke sharply. In unison they said, "Miss Sarah."

Sarah smiled. "Very good. This is my brother Joel." Several of the youngsters had already been eyeing him. He smiled at them uncertainly. "Could you tell me the names of the children, Morning Song?"

The Indian girl stood and put a hand on the sleek head of each child as she spoke. "This Dark River. This Spotted Dove, this Spotted Buckskin Girl. She is daughter of Chief Spotted Tail. Her Sioux name is Ah-ho-appa."

Sarah smiled at the musical names. "How lovely."

The names went on and on. How would she keep them all straight? "You'll have to help me for a few days until I can memorize them."

Morning Song nodded eagerly. "I very much like to help, Miss Sarah."

The day went well, with the children all eager to learn. Sarah was surprised at how quickly they picked up the English words.

"That was fun." Joel's face shone with enthusiasm. "I even learned some Sioux."

❧

Sarah was clattering around in the kitchen and Joel was out playing with Red Hawk when the front door banged open. "We're in the kitchen," Sarah called. She poured water from the wooden bucket into the kettle and set it on the stove as Rand came in.

Amelia rinsed the last of the breakfast dishes and dried her hands on her voluminous apron before untying it and draping it over the back of a chair. "I'm going to meet Jacob at the sutler's store. I'll be back for lunch." She smiled at Rand as she went out the door.

Sarah grabbed a coffee cup. "Want some coffee?"

"Yeah." He pulled out a chair and sat. "I wanted to hear about your first day of class."

She poured him a cup of coffee and handed it to him. "It was okay. Most of the little ones don't know any English, but there was an older teenager who speaks well. You'll get a chance to meet her if you stay a little while. Morning Song and Ah-ho-appa will be here anytime."

Rand curled his hands around his cup and frowned. "Be careful not to get too close to the Sioux, Sarah. You may be doing a lot of harm."

"Whatever do you mean? I would never hurt them."

"Maybe not intentionally. But have you thought about how they may become discontented with their lives as Sioux? If you give them too many different ideas, they may not fit in with their own people."

"That's ridiculous! Ah-ho-appa is a chief's daughter. Maybe she can help her people climb up out of the primitive way of life they lead." She jumped to her feet and took the steaming kettle off the stove. "You soldiers would have them stay in squalor. Rooster told Joel the only good Indian was a dead one!" She jerked her apron around her waist and tied it before she spun around to face him.

Rand sighed and ran his large hand through his hair. "A lot of the soldiers feel that way, but you surely don't believe I do. You know White Snake was one of my best friends back home." He and the Miami brave had been friends since Rand was five. "You're new out here, Sarah. There's a lot of prejudice and bitter feelings against Indians. You need to be careful about meddling in things you don't know anything about. I wish things were different. But I've seen too many Indian women taken advantage of in the short time I've been here. I wouldn't want anything to spoil Morning Song."

Sarah opened her mouth to defend herself, but there was a timid knock on the back door. She bit back the angry words and opened the door with a bright smile. She didn't want her friends to hear their discussion and think they shouldn't come back.

Morning Song peeked in the door, and Ah-ho-appa was behind her with timid, gentle eyes. Morning Song's black hair gleamed in the sunlight. Behind them Sarah heard Rand suck in his breath, presumably when he saw Morning Song's beauty.

"Miss Sarah, we are too early?" Morning Song dropped her gaze as Rand rose to his feet.

"I was just going. Think about what I said, Sarah." He smiled at the young women and strode out the door.

"You're just in time, Morning Song, Ah-ho-appa. The tea is ready." Sarah ignored Rand's departure. He hadn't given her a chance to explain her intentions. She wanted to show God's love to her Sioux friends. She swallowed her anger and poured them all a cup of tea.

Ah-ho-appa ran a gentle brown hand around the gold rim of Amelia's bone-thin china and sighed as she took an eager sip.

"What do we do today, Miss Sarah?" Morning Song asked.

"I thought we might go for a walk while the weather holds. Some of the men are predicting more cold weather within a few days, so we should take advantage of the sunshine while we can. I thought we might walk by the river."

Morning Song nodded. Her lovely face glowed with such joy and zest for life Sarah found all her angry thoughts fading away. She untied her apron and hung it on the peg by the door, then went to fetch her bonnet and cloak from the front hall.

The wind was a gentle whisper instead of its usual gale force. Mountain chickadees chittered in the trees along the riverbank, and the sound was soothing. The last few days had been unusually warm, above freezing for a change. Morning Song skipped along beside Sarah while Ah-ho-appa eagerly led the way. They passed several groups of soldiers felling trees for firewood, the heavy thunk of their axes comfortingly familiar.

For Sarah, it brought back memories of her father and brothers clearing the back pasture the summer before the war began. Those were happy days, days of laughter and contentment. In those days, Rand hurried over every evening after his work was done on the farm to take her for a buggy ride or just a walk by the river.

A small sigh escaped her, and Morning Song looked up, her face clouding. "Why are you so sad, Miss Sarah? Blue coat with holes in cheeks make you unhappy?"

Sarah smiled at her friend's reference to Rand's dimples. "How did you know that?"

"Your cheeks are red like an apple, and you look like this when I come in." Morning Song scowled. "Eyes sparkle like dew on leaf. Miss Sarah love blue coat?"

Sarah nodded. "Very much. But sometimes he makes me so mad."

"You marry blue coat?" Ah-ho-appa asked.

"I was engaged to him before the war, long before he ever met Jessica. But now he is going to marry Miss DuBois. Do you know what engaged is?"

Ah-ho-appa nodded. "Promised to marry. My mother wishes me to promise myself to Red Fox, but I say no. I want to marry blue coat and live in fine house like Miss Sarah's."

Sarah looked at her in dismay. "Oh, Ah-ho-appa, you don't mean that. It would be best for you to marry one of your own people."

"You think I am not good enough for blue coat?"

"You're a treasure, Ah-ho-appa. Any man would be lucky to have you. But it's complicated . . . You don't understand how hard it would be for you with a white man."

"My friend River Flower marry blue coat and live at edge of fort. She have baby boy."

Sarah knew she referred to the common-law marriage where the soldier paid the girl's father a few horses and "married" her. When he moved on to another fort, he generally left his woman and any children behind. "You deserve more than that. Those marriages aren't legal in the sight of the white man's laws. You should look for a man who will love and take care of you always."

Ah-ho-appa shook her head, her face set with determination. "I marry blue coat or no one." She turned and started back toward the cabin with Sarah trailing behind.

Morning Song looked at Sarah sadly. "I did not know Miss Sarah does not like our people." She turned and walked stiffly back toward the Indian encampment.

Sarah's heart sank as she followed the girl's erect figure. What had she done? And how was she going to fix it?

SEVEN

Smiling officers were decked out in their dress uniforms, their brass buttons and black boots shining. When Sarah arrived to the dance, she and Amelia were claimed for dances immediately. As an awkward lieutenant whirled her around the dance floor, Sarah found her gaze straying to Rand's dark head in the throng. He was so tall, he was easy to spot. His chin rested on Jessica's gleaming red head, and she was snuggled close to him. Sarah dragged her eyes away and forced herself to make polite conversation with poor Lieutenant Richards.

The evening became a blur as one officer after another claimed her for a dance. Would Rand ask her to dance? Such a foolish hope. Jessica wouldn't allow him out of her sight, she was sure. She danced twice with Isaac, Rand's bunky, then whirled on to the next soldier.

When there were only two more dances left, Jessica's father insisted on a dance with his daughter. Rand glanced Sarah's way, then made his way determinedly through the throng.

"Are you promised for this dance?" His voice was too polite.

"Not really. I don't think Joel will mind if he doesn't have to dance. I told him he had to dance with me so he could begin to learn. But his lesson will wait." She slid into his arms, and he guided her onto the floor.

She eyed his tense face. "You were right."

"About what?"

"Ah-ho-appa wants to marry a soldier and live in a home like mine. When I objected, she and Morning Song both thought I didn't think they were good enough to marry a white."

He nodded. "I'd heard Ah-ho-appa refused her father's choice for her. But don't beat yourself up over it. It may have happened anyway. There are a lot of Indian women who jump at the chance to take a soldier. And their families are well paid for them."

"That's awful!"

"I know, but it's the way things are out here. A woman doesn't have much value. Although as pretty as your friends are, they'll probably fetch a high price." His mouth twisted with distaste. "That will be a strong incentive to their fathers."

"Isn't there anything we can do?" Sarah couldn't stand the thought of her young friends sinking into that kind of life.

"Not really. Just be a friend to them. It's probably too late to do anything else."

The dance ended, and Rand escorted her to her chair. He stared down at her with a curious look on his face. It seemed almost tender. He opened his mouth but was interrupted by Jessica's arrival.

"There you are, darling," she cooed. "Be a dear and fetch me some punch."

"Of course. Would you care for some, Sarah?"

"No, thank you." She tensed as he walked away.

As soon as he was out of earshot, Jessica turned to her furiously. "Just what do you think you're going to accomplish by staying here? Why don't you just go home?"

Sarah forced a smile. "Jessica, we're just friends. And I'd like to be your friend too."

Confusion spread over Jessica's face, and she shook her head. "I have all the friends I need."

What more was there to say? "Very well."

Isaac Liddle approached the two women. "There's only one dance left." He extended his arm to Sarah. "May I?"

Rand was heading back, and the last thing she wanted was to be a hanger-on. She put her hand on his arm. "I'd be delighted."

He grinned down at her. "I know this might sound abrupt, Miss Sarah, but I figured I might as well throw my hat in the ring. With your permission, I'd really like to call on you."

Sarah hid her surprise. She'd seen Isaac hovering close over the past few weeks, but she had thought he was just being kind because he knew how hurt she'd been. "I don't know, Isaac. You're a good friend, and I'd hate to ruin our friendship."

"How could we ruin it? We could become even better friends."

Sarah was tempted. Isaac was a good Christian man and she had a lot of respect for him. "All right. But I can't make any promises."

He nodded. "I understand. Let's just get to know each other better and take it from there."

❧

The next morning, Ah-ho-appa was absent from school, and Morning Song refused to even look at Sarah. Sarah's heart ached as she saw the stiffness in her friend's demeanor. Everything seemed such a hopeless tangle.

"Don't go, Morning Song," she said as the Indian girl stood to go home. "I want to talk to you."

The girl almost seemed like her old self as she nodded and motioned her brother to go on without her.

"You seem to be avoiding me. I can't stand for you to be upset with me. Won't you please forgive me if I hurt you when we talked last? I really didn't mean I didn't think you were good enough for a soldier. Any man would be very lucky to marry you or Ah-ho-appa."

"I was very angry, but no more. I know you not wish to hurt me. And I have new friend."

Sarah's heart sank at the glow on the girl's lovely face. "A man?"

The girl nodded. "He is very handsome. Very light hair with eyes like a stormy sky."

Sarah tried to think of a soldier who fit that description, but she couldn't think of who it might be. "What's his name?"

"He is the new fur trader. Ben Croftner." Morning Song smiled a secret smile as she said his name.

Sarah stepped back as from a blow. "Oh, Morning Song. Not Ben. He's a very wicked, evil man." She caught the girl's arm. "Please, please stay away from him!"

Morning Song shook her hand off. "He told me you will say this. But he loves me. He is a good man. He offered my father five horses for me. We will marry tomorrow."

"Please, Morning Song. I beg you. Don't do this. It isn't a legal marriage. Ben won't stay with you."

The girl just gave her an angry stare and stalked off. "I thought my friend be happy for me, but I was wrong," she called back over her shoulder. "You are my friend no more."

Sarah clasped her hands and paced the floor. What

could she do? She couldn't just stand back and let Morning Song make a mistake like that. She caught up her cloak and hurried to the door. There just might be one hope.

She had borrowed a horse from the stables and found the trail leading to the trading post across the river. Isaac was crossing the parade ground, so she had asked him to escort her. He commandeered a private, and the two soldiers rode with her across the river.

The trading post was almost deserted when she arrived. A few Sioux hunkered around a fire in the front and looked up as they rode into the yard.

She slid off her horse and handed her reins to Isaac. "Wait for me here if you would."

He frowned. "I'm not sure you should go in alone."

"I'll be fine. He knows you're out here."

Labe was just coming out the door as she approached the building. "Sarah! What are you doing here?"

"I'd hoped you hadn't followed Ben out here, Labe. I need to see him. Is he here?"

He nodded. "He's in his office. I'll show you." He opened the door and led her across the dirt floor to a battered door. He rapped on it once, then swung it open for her.

Ben looked up when he heard the door open. "Sarah?" He rose to his feet eagerly, but his smile faded. His expression masked, he motioned for her to sit on the crate across from his crude table. "To what do I owe the honor of this call?"

"I want you to leave Morning Song alone." She didn't have time for any pleasantries, even if she was inclined to offer them, which she wasn't. "We both know you don't really care about her. She's too sweet for you to ruin."

He stroked his chin. "She'll be a lovely addition to my home, don't you think? And Indian women really know how to treat a man. I just don't see how I can agree with your request."

"Please, Ben. Don't do this." She leaned forward. "I can't bear to see her hurt."

"You're begging now, are you? Well, I might agree under one condition." He smiled gently. "You could take her place."

Sarah flushed. She should have known he'd suggest something like this. "You know how I feel about you."

He stood and thrust his hands into his pockets. "You're just angry, and I'm not saying you don't have a right to be. But anything I did was only because I loved you. And you haven't had any luck with Rand, now have you?"

"Maybe not, but I couldn't marry a man I couldn't trust." Sarah stood. There was no more to say. She loved Morning Song, but it was out of her hands.

"Then the wedding proceeds tomorrow as planned."

"You know it's not a real wedding! You'll just send her back to her family when you're tired of her."

Ben sneered. "She's just a savage, Sarah. That's all Indian women are good for."

"She's sweet and good. You'll take that and destroy it!"

"My, my, you do have an exalted opinion of me, don't you? Well, you just run on back to your precious Rand and let me take care of my own affairs. But don't think this is the last of our discussion." He caught her by the wrist and pulled her into a tight embrace. She fought to get away, but he pulled her closer and tipped her chin up. "I mean to have you, Sarah. One way or the other. Things will never be over between us."

When he released her, she dashed for the door. Isaac had dismounted. His gaze searched hers, and his lips tightened. "Did he hurt you?"

Her eyes burned, but she shook her head. "Let's go home."

❦

The next day Sarah watched the parade ground from the window as Ben arrived with five horses to take possession of his bride. In a beautifully beaded dress bleached to a pale yellow, Morning Song was seated on a horse almost the color of her dress. Her unbound hair, rippling past her waist, gleamed in the weak sunshine as she followed her new husband out of the fort. Sarah wept as she saw her friend's glowing face look back one last time.

The next day the weather made one of its drastic changes. The temperature plummeted, and the wind picked up. Then the blizzard Rooster had predicted struck in all its fury. The wind howled and blew snow through cracks around the windows. They all had to fight to keep the fires going in the fireplace. Jacob finally gave up the fight in the bedroom and dragged the bed and their belongings out into the kitchen.

They hung blankets over the doorway into the hall to try to block the flow of cold air. By the time the storm had vented its full fury, there were drifts of snow over the windows. Jacob opened the door only to be met with a column of snow completely covering the opening. They were effectively buried until the enlisted men dug them out. Sarah spent the day making loaves of bread while Amelia worked on a quilt. It was evening before they heard the scraping of shovels and friendly hellos from outside the door.

Sarah stood beside Jacob as he opened the door and two half-frozen men stumbled inside, their faces, beards, hair, and clothing all packed with snow.

"Glad to see you all are all right," the youngest private sputtered as he complied with Sarah's urging and took off his coat before staggering toward the fire. "The colonel said to tell you to stay inside tonight. We got a path dug out pert near all around the post so we can get from building to building. And the wood detail will be here with a load soon."

Amelia poured them all a cup of hot coffee and offered them bread and jam, which they accepted with alacrity. "Much obliged, ma'am." The young private got to his feet when the last crumb of bread was devoured. "We best be heading back to check with the colonel."

They saw their deliverers to the door and peered

out the narrow path left by their busy shovels. "It looks like a maze," Sarah said, unable to believe what she saw. The snow towered over twelve feet in many places. The narrow path trailed down the steps and around the corner toward Old Bedlam.

Jacob saw her shivering and shut the door. "You girls had better stay in until the weather breaks. Feels like it's at least twenty below. Exposed skin freezes in seconds in this kind of temperature."

❧

The weather didn't break for days. There would be a couple of days of bright sunshine, but the temperatures were way below zero, and the wind howled and blew the snow into ever-changing drifts. Those days would be followed by more snow and yet more snow. Sarah and Amelia took to pacing around the tiny quarters when Jacob and Rand were gone on duty. Jacob was sent out on telegraph duty several times, he was officer of the day three times, and he took his turn guarding the cattle and horse herds. They all tried to keep busy. Sarah played endless games of checkers with Joel and Amelia while Jacob and Rand saw to their duties.

Mail hadn't been able to get through either. Sarah longed for news from home. Surely Rachel had delivered the baby by now.

Jacob kept them informed of the goings-on at the post. Big Ribs had returned with the Corn band of Brulé ready to make peace. Then Man-Afraid-of-His-Horses trudged in with his band of Oglala. The winter had been hard on all of them.

Sarah was forced to discontinue the lessons with the Indian children. The weather was too cold for the little ones to be out, but she intended to start again in the spring. Her thoughts turned often to Morning Song. How was Ben treating her? She continued her lessons with Joel, in spite of his protests. But no amount of activity could distract her long from her worry about her friend.

EIGHT

The weather finally broke and with its usual capriciousness turned unseasonably balmy. Sarah slid a plate of eggs in front of Jacob. "I heard you tell Amelia you were going to the trading post today. Could I come along? I want to visit Morning Song."

He hesitated, then nodded. "I'll have to take a couple more men along for protection. Make sure you dress warm."

She hurried to do his bidding. About an hour later, she hurried across the open parade ground toward the stable. Jacob and Isaac, along with five other soldiers, were waiting with a mount for her, and they set off for the Indian encampment around the trading post.

The little settlement was full of Indians and trappers when they arrived. Sioux women stood around smoky fires patiently, but Sarah didn't see her friend. Isaac pointed out Ben's cabin, set off in a grove of trees by itself.

"I'll keep Ben busy," he promised.

Sarah dismounted and hurried toward the cabin. No one answered her first knock, so she rapped harder. Finally the door opened, and Morning Song peered around the door.

"Sarah," she gasped. She started to shut the door, but Sarah saw the marks on her face and pushed her way in.

"Oh, Morning Song," was all she could say for a moment. The young woman's face was marred by ugly purple and yellow bruises. One eye was swollen almost shut, and her lips were split and puffy. Morning Song cried softly as Sarah took her in her arms.

Morning Song pulled away and wiped at her eyes gingerly with the hem of her apron. "Do not look at me."

Sarah brushed the hair out of her friend's face.

"Why have you stayed? Didn't you know I would take you in?"

Morning Song lifted her hands, palms upward. "Ben is always watching me. He says if I leave, he will make me sorry. He says he will hurt you."

Sarah gathered the young woman back into her arms. "Don't you worry about Ben. He can't hurt me. The blue coats won't let him." She released her. "Get your buffalo robe and any possessions you want. You're coming with me."

When Morning Song was ready, Sarah opened the door cautiously and looked around. No one seemed to be paying any attention to the little cabin. "You stay in the trees. We'll meet you just over the knoll."

Morning Song nodded and slipped away soundlessly. Sarah hurried along the path and quickly mounted her horse. She told one of the soldiers to wait for Jacob while she took the others and started for home. Her heart pounded. If Ben looked out and saw her, he'd know for sure that something was up. She looked back as she rounded the bend. There was no hue and cry, so she began to breathe easier.

When she crested the knoll, she heard a scuffle and a cry to her right. "Morning Song," she called.

She urged her horse through the frozen brush with the soldiers following her. As she crashed through the thicket, she saw Morning Song struggling with a man. "Let go of her, Labe."

He looked up, his eyes startled. "Ben will have my hide," he whined. "I'm s'posed to see she doesn't get away. It's nothing to you, Sarah."

"Look at her, Labe. Go on. Look at her. Do you honestly think Ben has a right to beat her like that?"

Labe glanced at the Indian girl's battered face and dropped his eyes. "You know how Ben can be."

"I know. Now let go of her."

Labe's hand fell away, and Morning Song picked up her bundle and scurried toward Sarah. Sarah reached out a hand and helped her swing up on the back of her horse.

"Ben's going to be mad."

"You tell him to stay away from me and Morning Song." She nodded to the privates who had followed her, and they all crashed back through the thicket to the trail.

Isaac and the detachment were just rounding the crest of the knoll as they arrived. Isaac whistled when he saw Morning Song's face. "Ben do that?"

Sarah nodded, her lips tight. "Thanks for keeping him busy."

"No problem. We'd better hurry, though. He'll be after us any minute. He said something about going home for lunch. As soon as he sees she's missing, he's going to be hunting for her."

"He'll know where to look. Labe saw us." She quickly told him and Jacob the full story as they kicked their horses and galloped toward the safety of the fort.

When they reached the fort, Morning Song insisted on going to the Indian encampment. "I must see my father. He will wish to know."

Sarah and Jacob exchanged a long look. This could cause a major incident.

❧

Sarah helped Amelia hang up clothes on a line strung around the living room. The scent of lye soap stung her eyes, and she rubbed her reddened hands in the folds of her skirt. "I think I should go check on Morning Song. She should have been back by now. What if Ben waylaid her?"

"Jacob had a couple of soldiers watching. I don't

think he could get her." Amelia put on her cloak. "I'm going to the sutler's store for a few things. Want to come?"

She shook her head. "I want to wait here for Morning Song."

With the house empty, she paced the floor and waited. The cannon boomed as the soldiers went through the flag-lowering ritual. Maybe Ben was going to let Morning Song leave without protest.

Then a fist came down on the front door so hard that a picture on the wall by the door fell to the floor. Ben bellowed from the other side. Sarah picked up the picture. She just wouldn't answer. Maybe he'd go away. Her gaze went to the doorknob. She didn't remember locking it after Amelia left.

She looked around for a weapon, but nothing was in sight.

"Where is she?" he shouted.

Sarah bit her lip and said nothing. The doorknob began to turn, and she caught her breath as the door opened. Cold air rushed into the parlor, then Ben burst inside.

Sarah took a step back. "Get out of here, Ben. How dare you show your face here after what you did to Morning Song?"

His face reddened. "She is my property. No one complains if I discipline my horse, now do they? This is none of your business." He strode across the floor and caught her by the arms before she could even flinch away. He took her chin and tilted her head up as she struggled to get away. "I like it when you fight me," he whispered.

She stopped her struggling instantly, and he laughed again before releasing her. "Run away, little rabbit. But you won't escape me. I have plans for you."

Her pulse jumped in her throat. He was terrifying.

He leered at her, then stomped back out the door. "I'll find her, Sarah. She'll wish she'd stayed where she belonged. And you'll wish you'd stayed out of it."

Sarah let out a shaky breath as the door banged behind him. How had she ever thought he was attractive and kind? She shuddered. The door burst open again, and she flinched. But it was Rand.

"Are you all right?"

She nodded, close to tears. She hated to admit it, even to herself, but she was afraid of Ben. He was truly mad. "He's l-looking for Morning Song," she stammered, then burst into tears.

Rand crossed the room in one stride and pulled her into his arms. "It's all right, Green Eyes. We won't let him take her." He caressed her hair until the storm of weeping was past.

"I'm sorry," she gulped. "I don't know what came over me." She was very aware of his hand on her hair. That hand tightened on the back of her neck when she looked up.

Rand swallowed hard when she put a hand on his cheek. She searched his face and saw confusion mixed with a tenderness she'd hoped to find for weeks. "Rand," she began. But the door opened and Amelia rushed in. She'd heard the story at Suds Row.

Rand stepped away quickly, and the moment was lost. Again.

A
HEART'S
DANGER

ONE

EARLY MARCH 1866

The morning sun glinted on the patches of remaining snow as Sarah Montgomery hurried along to the Sioux encampment. Soldiers practiced in the big parade ground lined by fort buildings, and the sound of bugles pierced the cold air.

She rounded the last building and stopped in her tracks. An exodus of the Indian encampment was in full swing. Horses pulling travois of dismantled teepees and belongings packed the road north. She searched the throng for her friend Morning Song. There she was on a big buckskin. Sarah waved and called her name.

Morning Song slid from the horse's back and met her at the end of the procession. She was fully recovered from the beating she'd taken from the hands of her so-called "husband" in November.

Sarah hugged her. "What's happening? Where are your people going?"

"We go to meet up with Big Ribs. The elders were all too ready to talk of war after what Ben did." There was no lilt, no joy in Morning Song's voice. "I cannot stay here. Ben will find me if I remain."

The wind blew across the parade grounds, and Sarah shivered. "But you're safe here. The soldiers will protect you now."

Morning Song released her and stepped back. "I must go with my people. Thank you for all you have done for me, Sarah. I will never forget you."

A lump formed in Sarah's throat. "That sounds like good-bye."

"I hope to see you again, my friend, but . . ." Morning Song looked down. "I fear our people will be at war soon."

"We will always be friends, Morning Song."

The young woman nodded. "My mother waits. I must go." She hugged Sarah again, then pulled herself up onto the horse's bare back and rode to join the line of moving horses.

Sarah watched them go with a profound sense of sadness. At least Morning Song was out of Ben's clutches. When she came back, perhaps her spirit would have healed from his abuse.

When Sarah turned, she nearly ran into Rand Campbell. His big hands came down on her shoulders to steady her, and she looked up into his handsome face. A muscle twitched in his square jaw, and there was no sign of his dimples. She found it hard to read him these days.

She stepped away. "Sorry I nearly ran you down."

His arms fell to his sides. "A tiny thing like you couldn't knock me down. Are you okay?"

She nodded. "I'm sad to see her go, but at least Ben won't be able to touch her." With a parting smile, she turned toward the quarters she shared with Jacob and Amelia.

The impermanence of her situation gnawed at her. Isaac Liddle seemed to care about her and her little brother Joel, and she suspected he would propose soon. Even though she craved a place of her own, there seemed no real haven for her. She still couldn't contemplate a future without Rand in it, but she had to figure it out. He was going to marry Jessica, and she had to accept it.

───※───

Snow flurries skated across the landscape as Ben Croftner crossed Fort Laramie's parade ground and stomped toward the Sioux encampment. The wind poked icy fingers through his thick coat and tried to tear the hat from his head, but he barely noticed the glowering clouds overhead. He had more important things to do this morning than worry about the weather.

Just let those savages try to stop him from taking Morning Song. His fingers curled into his palms with the desire to smash a face or two. Although the face he really wanted to destroy was Lieutenant Rand Campbell's. As he walked in front of the officers' quarters, someone called his name. He turned to see a red-haired woman waving to him. Her pale skin was flawless, and her full lips turned up in an alluring smile.

Her lashes fluttered in a come-hither way. "Mr. Croftner."

She certainly was beautiful, if you liked the type. Cool and remote. He stopped at the steps and smiled at her. "At your service. I believe I've heard of you. You are Miss Jessica DuBois, correct?"

"I am. Won't you come in, Mr. Croftner? I think we have something in common."

He allowed his gaze to sweep over her until she flushed. "And what would that something be?"

She lifted her chin and her smile evaporated. "We both want to keep Sarah Montgomery away from Rand Campbell." She took a step back toward the door. "Won't you join me for some tea?"

Morning Song could wait. He followed her inside to a large parlor with a soft flowered carpet on the wood floor. Delicate tables flanked a horsehair sofa and three chairs completed the furnishings. Garden pictures and gold sconces adorned two walls while the fireplace dominated the third. The dining room was through an arched doorway.

A young, attractive black woman hovered in the doorway, and Jessica glanced at her. "Bring us some tea, please, Rose."

Rose nodded and walked out of his sight.

Jessica indicated one of the chairs. "Have a seat, Mr. Croftner." When he shrugged out of his coat and sank into the comfortable chair, she settled on the sofa and arranged the folds of her green dress. "I have a plan."

As she explained her plan, he began to smile. It was superior in every way to his own. Sarah would learn his vengeance was terrible.

He crossed his legs. "Tell me more."

Rand paused with his group at the North Platte River Bridge. He could see miles in all directions across the plains so it should be safe for the night. He waved to his brother Jacob. "We'll spend the night here so we're ready to restring wire for the telegraph in the morning."

Jacob nodded and dismounted. He was shorter than Rand and stockier, with dark-brown hair and eyes, but no one was able to miss the clear resemblance between them. He ordered the soldiers to set up camp. Rand pulled the saddle off Ranger and broke some of the ice in the river so the horses could drink. He heard a shout and looked up to see a group of fifteen Sioux, faces painted, charging across the river toward them with shrill war cries.

Rand dove for his rifle. He lined the sight of the Henry up to his eye and trained it on a young warrior. Rand's finger paused on the trigger as he saw the youth's face. He was probably only fifteen, although he looked like he'd seen battle before—he had a livid scar running down one cheek. The boy stared at him defiantly as Rand put pressure on the gun's trigger.

Rand shook his head and lowered his rifle long enough for the boy to lift his spear in his hand and wheel around with a bloodcurdling yell.

"That there was a mighty big mistake, young feller." Rooster had seen the exchange. "You'll likely run into him again, and he won't be so charitable-like."

Rooster was probably right. But the warrior had reminded him of his youngest brother, Shane. The same careless free spirit. Rand just couldn't kill him.

※

The weather turned frigid and stayed that way. Days went by with no relief. Finally, the colonel announced a party at Old Bedlam. Rand tried to keep his distance from Sarah, but his gut tightened every time she swept by in Isaac Liddle's arms with her heart-shaped face turned up to his admiring glance. It was ridiculous to care that his friend was courting her, but Rand couldn't help the stab of jealousy that pierced his chest when he realized she'd likely marry Isaac.

Halfway through the party, a sentry rushed in. "Colonel, Spotted Tail is at the Platte!"

Colonel Maynadier jumped up and clapped his hat atop his thinning blond hair. "Raise the white flag and get my horse ready." He turned to Rand. "Lieutenant, I hate to drag you away from the festivities, but I need you to accompany me. We'll ride out to meet Spotted Tail and assure him of our good intentions. This is what I've been waiting and hoping for. He's been with Red Cloud. If Spotted Tail is ready for peace, perhaps Red Cloud is too."

Rand nodded. "I'll meet you at the corral, sir."

He followed the colonel and the other officers to the corral and got their horses. At least they were all dressed in their finest. It would show respect to the Sioux. The wind picked up as he swung atop Ranger's black back and the officers got into formation. They went out to meet the column of Sioux amassing over the rise. The wind carried the chanting to them.

Frowning, the colonel reined in his horse. "Sounds like a death lament."

Rand's gut tightened. Could Spotted Tail have died? He waited with the rest of the officers by the fort gate as the lament grew louder.

As the tribe drew nearer, he saw Spotted Tail's face drawn with grief, so the deceased wasn't the chief himself. Spotted Tail's horse dragged a travois with a shrouded body. Rand stared hard at the covered pack, but could see no hint of the victim. His fingers tightened on the reins as a messenger rode forward.

The Sioux warrior wheeled on his pinto, then went and stopped in front of Maynadier. "Chief Spotted Tail wishes to bury his daughter in the white man's cemetery. As Ah-ho-appa drew near death, she asked her father to bring her back here. Shall you honor this request?"

Rand inhaled and glanced over at his brother. This would hit Sarah hard.

The colonel inclined his head. "I would be honored to have his daughter in the white man's cemetery."

The warrior wheeled again and rode back to the

rest of the tribe. Rand couldn't hear what he said to Spotted Tail, but the chief urged his horse forward until he reached the colonel. He stopped close enough for Rand to see Ah-ho-appa's face.

Colonel Maynadier put his hand on his chest. "My heart grieves at your loss, my friend. I hope we can be at peace with your people now."

Tears welled up in Spotted Tail's eyes. "My heart is very sad, and I cannot talk on business. I will wait and see the counselors."

"Of course, my friend."

Rand fell in with the troops as they rode back to the corral. He didn't want to think of Sarah's grief. He shouldn't care so much about seeing her hurt, but heaven help him, he still did.

Back at the fort Jacob dismounted, then went to grab Ranger's halter. "You should be the one to tell Sarah."

TWO

The dance was long over by the time Rand got to the quarters where Sarah lived with Jacob and Amelia. Sarah sat stitching on quilting material in her lap when Rand strode into the parlor. The lamplight cast a soft glow over her glorious red-gold hair, and he caught his breath. She seemed to get lovelier all the time.

He cleared his throat. "Sarah?"

She looked up, and her green eyes widened as he stepped closer. "What's wrong?"

He'd never been able to hide his emotions from her. "I don't quite know how to tell you except to just say it." He took off his hat and raked a hand through his hair. "It's Ah-ho-appa. She's dead, Sarah. Pneumonia." He cleared his throat. "It's been a hard winter, not enough food. She was too weak to fight the lung infection."

Sarah stared at him. "No, not Ah-ho-appa." She reached up and grabbed his hand. "You must be wrong."

He squeezed her hand gently. "I'm sorry. I know you loved her."

Sarah shook her head. "There must be some mistake."

"There's no mistake. I saw her myself. Her father has asked for her to be buried in the soldier cemetery. He said she wanted to marry a soldier."

Sarah put her face in her hands and wept. "It's all my fault. If she hadn't been friends with me, she would have been content with her life. She would have married some young warrior who would have taken care of her."

Rand took her hands and drew her to her feet and into his arms. "I'm sorry, Sarah, but you did all you could for her. At least she didn't go through what

Morning Song did." Rand held her until her weeping was over. "The funeral's tomorrow. I'll take you if you want."

She lifted her wet face and nodded. "I must tell her parents how much I loved her."

Rand couldn't tear his gaze from her face. He'd always loved her compassion for other people. She was as beautiful inside as she was on the outside.

Several hundred mourners, consisting of Indians, off-duty soldiers, Colonel Maynadier, as well as Major O'Brien, who had arrived to take over command of Fort Laramie, crowded the parade ground at sunset for the funeral.

Sarah stood with Amelia in the cemetery. The scaffold beside them rose eight feet in the air. The soldiers had built it to hold the coffin to honor Ah-ho-appa. She couldn't tear her horrified gaze away from the heads and tails of two white ponies hanging from the structure.

Amelia, her dark hair tucked into a bonnet, looked that direction and grimaced. "Jacob said the ponies were her favorites, and they were killed to carry her into the afterlife. Their heads are pointed toward the rising sun." She gestured to a barrel of water. "That's to quench their thirst before they begin their ride."

Sarah shuddered and hugged herself. "It seems so barbaric."

She watched the ambulance bring the coffin. A mountain howitzer followed the ambulance. The post band played a solemn march as the Brulé Sioux with Spotted Tail circled the scaffold. Behind them marched most of the men of the garrison, and they formed a large square around the Sioux.

Her gaze touched on Isaac Liddle's open and honest face. She didn't know if she could ever feel as strongly about him as she did Rand, but she had to move on with her life. Somehow.

Officers transported the girl from the ambulance into the open coffin. Colonel Maynadier contributed a pair of gauntlets to keep Ah-ho-appa's hands warm. Rand added red flannel and Jacob put a pair of moccasins into the coffin.

The Sioux women walked to the coffin. Each whispered something to Ah-ho-appa and dropped a small gift inside. When the women were done, Sarah approached and gazed down into her friend's casket, built by the fort's carpenter. Her long, raven-black hair was braided with bright-red ribbons and lay draped over her shoulders and across the soft white elk skin that covered her.

Tears filled Sarah's eyes. "Good-bye, my friend." She dropped one of her brooches into the casket.

The colonel had arranged for both Sioux and Christian funerals. When the ceremonies were over, Sarah pushed through the crowd while Rand followed her.

"That was a nice thing to do," he whispered. "You've probably made a friend for life. I know it's hard for you, Sarah. It's all so different out here. You're used to activity and fun. It's pretty dreary confined to those small rooms all the time and never being allowed to go outside the fort. If the weather holds, how about going skating on the Laramie River tomorrow after worship services?"

Sarah nodded eagerly. Could he really want to spend some time with her, or was he just sorry for her?

"Jessica's been wanting to go for weeks."

Sarah's heart clenched. He didn't seem to hear her quick intake of breath as he offered his arm and escorted her back to her quarters. He'd made it clear where his loyalties were.

✦

Sunday morning was bright and sunny, with the mercury hovering near twenty-five degrees though it was already March. Shouts of laughter and squeals echoed through the trees as Sarah laced her skates. She'd worn her warmest dress over a pair of Joel's trousers. Her brother was already out on the ice with his friends, and she smiled as he went zipping by with his blond hair flying in the wind.

Rand skated by with Jessica laughing up at him, and Sarah's heart squeezed. She got up and tucked her hands into mittens, then skated along the frozen surface of the river. She refused to let the circumstances spoil her day. Rand was going to marry Jessica, and she was determined to be fine with it.

She linked hands with Amelia and skated until Jacob came to claim his wife for a race. Her chest burned from exertion so she skated over to rest on a rock where she'd left her boots. The cold seeped into her skin after a few minutes, and she stood to warm up. There was a movement in the trees, and she squinted at the shadows.

Was that Jessica talking with Ben?

Something about their furtive behavior made her frown. She hadn't seen Ben since Ah-ho-appa's funeral, though she'd half expected him to accost her when she was out and about.

She wished she could hear what they were talking about. She stared at her skates. If she took them off, she might be able to move more silently in their direction. And where was Rand? Did he know his fiancée was with Ben?

She sat back down on the rock and untied her skates, then slipped them off. With her boots on, she moved as quietly as she could into the trees. The deep timbre of Ben's voice grew plainer as she leaned against a tree and strained to hear.

"I have the plan in place."

"I knew you were the right man to talk to." Jessica's words could just be made out over the wind. "I just want her out of the way. You won't hurt her, will you? Rand would never forgive me."

"Of course not. I only want the best for her myself."

Who were they talking about? Sarah wished she

dared to get closer, but she'd certainly be discovered. She tipped her ear toward the voices again.

"There's no great rush as long as you get it done," Jessica said.

"I'll get it done."

Footsteps came closer, and Sarah would be found if she lingered. If only she knew who they were talking about. Ben never wanted anyone's good but his own, so she feared for whomever he had in his sights next.

⁂

Rand glanced around the throng of people skating along the Laramie River. Jessica had been here just a few minutes ago, but she had disappeared, probably chatting with an admirer or two. Most of the soldiers envied him his fiancée, but he was beginning to weary of her constant jealousy about Sarah.

He saw a flash of blue on his left and turned to see Sarah skating toward him. Her green eyes held confusion, and she looked away when she saw him.

He skated to meet her and offered her his arm. "Care to skate with me? Jessica is nowhere to be found."

She bit her lip, then put her hand on his arm. "Of course."

Tendrils of her red-gold hair had escaped their pins and curled around her face. Maybe this hadn't been such a good idea, but he wanted to be polite since she was alone. They pushed off from the shore and joined the skaters in the middle of the river.

"Where's Jessica?" she asked after a long moment.

"I'm not sure. Maybe her mother wanted to talk to her."

"I don't think so."

He wasn't sure about the tone in her voice. Was that a challenge? "Did you see her?"

She shot a glance at him. "How well does she know Ben?"

He frowned. "Ben? I don't think she's met him at all."

She stumbled a little as she skated. "This is probably none of my business."

"It's a little late now. You saw her with Ben?"

She nodded and pointed with a mittened hand. "Back in the trees. They were talking about some plan."

"What plan?"

"I don't know. They didn't say, but they seemed to be well acquainted."

"I'll ask her about it. I don't like her spending any kind of time with Croftner. Maybe she doesn't know how many lies he's told and how he's wrecked my life."

She stopped in the middle of the river and grasped both his hands in hers. "Did he ruin your life, Rand? When you say it like that, I almost hear regret in your voice."

He wished he could forget about the way their hearts had seemed knit together by the Almighty. Forget the way her hair smelled and the way her lips tasted.

THREE

R and walked Jessica home in the twilight. Her cheeks were red from the cold, and her eyes sparkled. And no wonder. Nearly every soldier on the river had asked her to skate with him. He found he didn't have a speck of jealousy about it either.

Seeing Sarah with Isaac was another matter.

He stopped on her porch and pressed her hand. "I'll be gone tomorrow for a few days. I have wood detail."

She gave a pretty pout. "I'll miss you."

"Will you?" He stared down at her. Would she tell him the truth if he asked her about her conversation with Ben?

She tipped her head to one side. "Why are you looking at me like that? Do I have a smudge on my cheek?"

"I didn't know you knew Ben Croftner."

Her eyes widened. "I know everyone at this post, Rand. Surely you're not jealous. Papa asked me to deliver a message to Ben if I saw him. He was at the river so I did as my father asked. Was that wrong?"

"Of course not."

She was lying. He could see it in the way she cast her gaze at her boots, then looked back up at him with a calculated smile. She was so used to using her beauty to blind the men around her.

"Ben lied about me many times. I don't like him, and I don't trust him. I'd rather you never speak to him."

Color tinged her cheeks. "Very well, if you're going to pout about it. I'll tell my father to deliver his own message next time."

He squeezed her mittened hand. "Ben hurts anyone he comes in contact with. I don't want you to be one of his casualties."

Her expression cleared and she laughed, then went

up on her toes to brush a kiss over his cheek. "I love it when you're possessive. There's no one I want but you, Rand."

He released her hand. "I'll see you when I get back."

Her eyes were hurt and questioning as she turned to go inside. He had handled that badly. It wasn't her fault he hadn't realized there was more to a happy marriage than similar goals.

❧

Two days later the afternoon sun warmed Rand's face as he led a detachment into the forest for wood. It had to be close to seventy degrees, and winter had given up without a murmur. Pools of water and mud stood where snowbanks had once piled.

They had four huge stacks of wood cut and were about to load it onto the mules and travois when loud yells sounded from down in the ravine to their right.

"Injuns!" Rooster grabbed his rifle and vaulted onto his horse.

There was a wild scramble as the rest of the men clambered onto their mounts and followed Rooster's mad charge.

"There's only three of them," Rand muttered as he fell into line. But the rest of the Sioux were hiding. As the main force leaped out from behind bushes and rocks, the charge of the cavalry faltered. Instead of three, there were at least twenty-five.

"It's a trap," Captain Brown shouted. "Retreat! Retreat!"

But Rand was in the front line, and retreat would invite an arrow in the back. He slid off his horse and flung himself down behind a boulder. He took aim and began shooting desperately, pushing away the reality of his own situation. He would get his company safely away, then he'd worry about how to get out himself.

Rooster wheeled around on his horse and fired at a group of Sioux crouching behind a rock. "Git out of there, boy! It's better to say 'here's where he ran' than 'here's where he died.'" When Rand kept firing, Rooster swore, then galloped away, still shouting for Rand to run.

Something bit into his flesh, and Rand grabbed his shoulder. His fingers dripped with blood when he pulled his hand away. A bullet? But these Indians just seemed to have bows and arrows. He heard another shot off to his left and felt a fiery sting on his left temple. Then darkness claimed him.

When Rand awoke he was lying beside a fire. He groaned and tried to move, but his hands and feet were bound.

"So you're finally awake."

He looked up at the familiar voice. Croftner? Here? Where were the Indians? He shook his head to clear it. He must still be asleep. But a hard boot in his ribs convinced him he wasn't dreaming.

"So we meet again, old friend." Ben stooped and sneered in his face. A lock of white-blond hair fell across his gray eyes. "Did you really think I'd let you get away with taking my girl? But I'm going to do worse to you, Campbell. When I get through with you, you'll wish that bullet had killed you outright."

"How—how did you get me away from the Indians?"

Ben smiled, but the expression was a cruel one. "I paid them to stage an attack. They were just Laramie loafers out for enough money to buy some liquor." He leaned forward and spat in Rand's face. "Are you ready to die, Campbell? You'll pray for death before I'm through with you." His lips twisted.

Rand held his gaze. "You can't frighten me with heaven, Ben."

Ben gaped at him, then stood with an angry oath.

"Don't tell me you've gotten religion," he jeered. "If that doesn't beat all! Hey, Labe, Rand thinks he's going to heaven." He sneered and spat on the ground. "But he's going to find out what hell's really like before we're through."

Rand turned his head as Labe shuffled from behind a rock. Labe's dirty-blond hair fell across his face as he fastened his suspenders. "Sorry to see you're mixed up in this, Labe." Labe's pale-blue eyes widened, but he said nothing.

Ben laughed again, an ugly laugh with no mirth in it. "'Too bad you're mixed up with this, Labe,'" he mimicked. He tossed a shovel toward his younger brother. "Get digging."

Labe cast one agonized glance toward Rand's prone figure, then picked up the shovel and began to dig a small hole. He took a stake out of the knapsack beside the fire and pounded it into the hole, all the while keeping his eyes averted from Rand's gaze.

Rand realized what Ben was planning. He was going to stake him out in the sun. A slow death, but a sure one with no water. The nights would be cold too, even if the days were warm. All he could do was pray he died with dignity.

A few minutes later Labe finished his task and threw the shovel down, then wiped the sweat from his face with his sleeve. "I'm done, Ben." He glanced at Rand, then looked away.

"I'm not blind. Grab his feet." Ben grabbed Rand by his wounded arm, and the men dragged him toward the two posts.

Rand clenched his teeth to keep from crying out from the pain. Beads of sweat broke out on his forehead as he fought to retain consciousness.

Ben knelt and wrapped a strip of rawhide around Rand's left wrist. "Don't just stand there—help me, you fool," he snapped.

Labe shuffled forward and knelt at Rand's feet. Ben grinned as he wound rawhide strips around Rand's other wrist. "Think of me with Sarah as you're lying out here, old friend. Stage two of my plan is being put into action right now. Your little fiancée won't be too thrilled with this part of the plan, but her plan for Sarah was pure genius."

"What are you talking about?" Rand groaned as his wounded arm was wrenched above his head and bound to the stake.

"Your little missy cooked up a pretty good scheme

to help me get Sarah. It's really what gave me the idea for this little rendezvous."

So this was the plan Sarah had heard them talking about. He should have dug into this more. "What about Sarah?"

"You just stew about it while you're dying. But you can go knowing I'll take good care of Sarah."

Labe tied Rand's ankles to the stakes, then stood up, dusting his hands.

"If you leave me here, Labe, you'll never get my blood off your hands," Rand whispered.

"Shut up." Ben kicked him in the side, then turned to his brother. "Get our things and let's get going."

Labe's mouth worked soundlessly, and he hesitated. For an instant Rand thought he was going to defy his brother, but in the end, Labe dropped his head and shuffled off to obey Ben.

The two brothers swung onto their horses and looked down at Rand lying spread-eagled on the rocky ground. "So long, Campbell." Ben's smile was triumphant. "The best man always wins, you know. You were never ruthless enough."

Rand watched as they rode off, biting down on the pleading words struggling to escape. Wouldn't

Croftner love it if he begged for mercy? He turned his head away from the direct glare of the sun and began to pray against whatever they had cooked up for Sarah.

※

After two days with no water, Rand was delirious. He muttered incoherently, sometimes shouting, sometimes screaming. The nights were bad too. The warm spring days plunged into cold nights and he shuddered with the cold.

At one point he realized he was quoting the twenty-third Psalm. "'Yea, though I walk through the valley of the shadow of death, I will fear no evil.'" He was surprised he still remembered it after all these years. He'd learned it at his grandma's knee when he was eight. But this was the valley of the shadow of death, and somehow, he wasn't afraid to die. Something inside kept him from giving into the fever that racked his body.

The morning of the third day, he awoke relatively clearheaded after a rough night. His lips felt thick and his tongue filled his mouth. Today he would probably die. But at least he could see the land he loved with clear eyes one last time. His eyes closed several times, but he forced them open. This time when he fell asleep, he didn't think he would ever awaken. But the lack of water began to take a heavy toll, and he slipped into delirium for what must be the last time. His final thought was of Sarah, and he prayed for God to watch over her.

FOUR

Rand cried out and thrashed as the cooling night woke him, shivering as the chill breeze swept over him. He vaguely remembered a dark face swimming before his eyes off and on. Someone forcing water down his parched throat. He tried to move and found his hands and feet were unbound. He looked to his right and saw that Ranger was tied to a tree nearby.

He sat up slowly, his head spinning. Beside him lay a skin plump with water. He took it and drank greedily, then wiped his mouth. A buffalo robe covered the lower half of his body. Puzzled, he looked around. Who had cut him free? He frowned and tried to concentrate on the dark face at the edge of his memory, but nothing more would come.

Where were Ben and Labe? He looked around slowly as his head continued to clear. The sun lay low in the sky. Only an hour or so of daylight was left. He swallowed another swig of water and shook his head to clear it, then stood. He swayed, then staggered toward his horse.

His mouth watered at the sight of jerky slung over his saddle. He stuffed some into his mouth as he leaned his head against Ranger's flank. Fortified with food and water, he forced himself to swing up into the saddle. He swayed and caught at the pommel to steady himself. He had to make it. Sarah depended on it. He remembered what Ben had said about Jessica, and he had to get back to make sure Sarah was all right. And Jessica. Surely she couldn't be involved with a man like Croftner. Ben had to have said that to upset him.

He urged Ranger to a trot and clung tightly to avoid slipping out of the saddle. Within an hour he was in familiar territory. Maybe he could make Fort

Laramie before it was fully dark. But his horse was exhausted, and he was forced to walk. Rand was still weak from his ordeal, and he had to stop often to catch his breath. He stopped for the night on a bluff about five miles southwest of the fort. Barely conscious, he crawled into his bedroll and closed his eyes.

❧

The weather had warmed to the seventies the last few days. Sarah snatched her bonnet and handed Amelia's to her. "I'm tired of being cooped up. Let's go for a stroll in the sunshine." Amelia followed her into the bright sunshine. Puddles stood in the parade ground, and she stopped to listen to the band practicing.

Her bonnet shaded the glare from her face, and she glanced around. The men should be back from woodcutting detail soon. She noticed Amelia's perusal of her face. "What?"

"You'll have to make a decision about Isaac soon, Sarah. Are you going to marry him if he asks you?"

Sarah pressed her lips together and started off toward the sutler's store. "I don't know. I like him. He's so kind to Joel. And Joel likes him too. That's important to me." She kicked a rock out of her path. "Nothing is as I thought it would be when I came out here. I thought Joel and I would have a home. You and Jacob have been wonderful, but you haven't been able to really settle into married life, not with the two of us living in that tiny space with you both. I should just marry Isaac."

"You don't love him, though."

She cast a sidelong glance at her friend who knew her too well. "Not yet, but I hope to. I can't pine after Rand the rest of my days. He's made his decision very clear."

"I think he regrets his decision."

"I doubt it." Her words died as she saw Jessica waving to them from in front of the store.

"Sarah, Amelia." She was dressed in a cream percale gown lavished with cream lace. Her red hair hung to her shoulders and gleamed in the sunshine. "I was hoping to find you. I haven't seen much of you lately. Isaac has arranged for a detachment to escort Mother and me on a picnic. Would you like to come?"

Sarah glanced at Amelia, who looked as confused as Sarah felt. "Why? You've made no secret of how you feel about me all winter. Why the sudden change of heart?"

Jessica smiled and reached out to touch Sarah's arm. "I realized how petty I was being. You're part of Rand's past, and I'd like us to be friends. Can't we start over? The fort is too small for enmity between us."

Sarah was silent a moment. The jibe about being part of Rand's past stung, but it was true. It was time to let go and heal as many relationships as possible. Besides, she was weary of the tiny area she was allowed. It would be grand to see some new terrain. That was the one thing she hadn't accepted about fort life yet. The restrictions. Back home she was used to going for long rides by herself, wandering in the woods, or just walking along a country road. Now she was not allowed off the fort premises without a guard of at least five soldiers. And it seemed the fort's parade ground got smaller and smaller every day.

Sarah hoped her smile looked genuine. "That sounds lovely. We'll go pack some food."

Jessica patted her arm, then tugged her forward along the wooden walk, Amelia and Mrs. DuBois not far behind. "Don't bother. Mother has packed enough for an entire troop."

Jessica chatted easily as they strolled to the stable. Isaac had their mounts waiting for them, already cinched with sidesaddles. He helped Sarah up, and she smiled into his hazel eyes. Such a kind man. Why couldn't she feel more strongly about him? She'd sensed his impatience at the way she kept him at a distance. She expected a proposal from him at any time.

The women followed the detail of twelve soldiers west toward the purple mountains.

Jessica kept up her smiling chatter, and gradually Sarah relaxed. Was it too much to hope that Jessica might be like this all the time? They found a grassy area near an outcropping of rocks and spread out their blankets away from any melting snowdrifts. The air was pungent with the scent of sage, and the purple mountains in the distance reached up to kiss the blue skies.

After lunch Isaac knelt beside Sarah. "I'd like to bring down some game while we're out here." His soft gaze searched hers, as if trying to determine if she was open to a more serious conversation.

Sarah looked away. "Of course. We'll accompany you."

She gathered up the picnic things, then mounted with the other women. Sarah let her horse pick its way up the winding trail, breathing in the scent of sage.

She reveled in the sense of freedom from the confines of Fort Laramie.

As the men listened with rapt attention to Jessica's story about a ball in Boston, Sarah let her horse walk farther and farther away from them. Even Amelia didn't notice. At the top of the bluff, she slid off her horse and sat where she could look at the fort below her. She chuckled at Isaac's sudden agitation when he discovered she was missing.

She raised a hand and opened her mouth to call to him when her horse whinnied behind her. She stood quickly and turned to see an Indian warrior, heavily painted, galloping toward her. She froze in terror, then tried to put her foot into the stirrup to mount.

But the Indian was upon her in an instant. He leaned down and scooped her up, his horse barely pausing as he caught her.

Sarah struggled to get away, gagging at the odor of bear grease and sweat, but his arm was like a steel band around her waist. She screamed, certain she was doomed. But the crack of a rifle sounded and the Indian slumped against her, his arm loosening.

She wrenched free and fell from the horse. Stunned from the swiftness of both the attack and her rescue, she lay on the hard ground as the Indian wheeled away, his face glazed with pain, holding a hand to his bloody shoulder.

Rooster galloped out of a stand of trees, his cavalry cap gone and spiky red hair standing on end. "What's wrong with you, gal? Don't you got no sense atall?" He slid off his horse and pulled her to her feet. "Git on that horse now!" He shoved her up into the saddle. "There's prob'ly more of them sneakin' varmints around. We gotta git to the fort." He slapped her horse's rump, and they started down the bluff.

Isaac, Mrs. DuBois, and Amelia, with the rest of the soldiers, met them at the bottom. Isaac's face was tight with anger. But before he could say anything, they heard a whoop behind them and turned to see a group of Indians charging toward them.

"Get going!" Isaac fell back and fired at the Indians to give Rooster time to get the girls to the safety of the fort.

Amelia and Sarah kicked their horses into a mad dash for the fort as Mrs. DuBois screamed and moved faster than Sarah had ever seen. Jessica kicked her horse into a gallop, her face calm, and the rest of the soldiers brought up the rear.

A bullet whistled by Sarah's head as she clung to the horse's back. Then her horse stumbled and she catapulted into a thorny bush. Her skin was pierced in a dozen places, and she lay there too stunned to even move.

A young warrior galloped up, brandishing a knife. Before she could even think to scream, he cut her loose from the thornbush and hauled her up in front of him.

Sarah tried to struggle away, but her head was throbbing from the fall and soon darkness descended.

The next morning Rand awoke ravenous. His sunburn still throbbed, but he was stable. His store of food was all gone, and his ammunition was low, so he took his rifle and made his way down to the river. It wasn't long before he shot a jackrabbit. It was tough and stringy as he ate it hot from the spit, but it would do. At least it would give him the strength he needed to get back.

He saddled up Ranger and swung up into the saddle. In spite of the deceptive distances, he knew he'd be home soon. The fort drew nearer very quickly.

Now he could make out the individual buildings. There was the commissary and the stable. The barracks and the hospital. Was he too late to help Sarah? He urged Ranger into a gallop.

He arrived about eight o'clock. There seemed to be an uncommon amount of activity as dozens of soldiers jostled one another in their hurry to catch a mount and saddle up. Rooster, his voice shrill with emotion, called for a fresh horse.

His heart pounding, Rand spotted Jacob and Isaac saddling horses beside the post headquarters. He kicked his mount into a canter and pulled up beside them. "What's going on?"

Jacob's voice was grim. "Indians got Sarah."

The clipped words hit Rand like a blow. He felt light-headed with shock. "When?" He'd been worried about Ben and Jessica's plan, and he should have been praying for safety from the Sioux.

"This morning. We're just back for fresh horses and supplies. You coming?"

"Let me get a fresh mount." Outwardly he was calm, but inwardly a cauldron of emotion was churning. Anger, guilt, love. He realized in a blinding instant what a fool he'd been. He'd never be able to ignore his feelings for her. He and Sarah had something precious, and he had treated it as something of inconsequence. And now it might be too late. He shuddered at the thought of what Sarah had perhaps already endured. He followed Isaac and Jacob out of the fort as they caught up with Rooster on his way to pick up the trail.

Just before dusk they found a spot where a large group of horses had trampled the ground. Rand knelt in the dust. "Some of these prints belong to white men. Look here, Isaac. Shod hoof prints and boot heels."

Isaac knelt beside him and touched the prints. "Looks like two, maybe three, men."

Rooster came up behind them. "Sure am glad to see you, boy. You look bad, though. Yer skin's blistered and peeling. What happened to you? How'd you git away from them Injuns?"

"I'll tell you later." Finding Sarah was more important.

Rooster nodded and knelt beside them. "What'd ya find, boys?"

Rand gestured to the boot prints. "What do you make of this, Rooster? What would white men be doing with a pack of Sioux?"

Rooster studied the ground for a moment. "Don't

look too good, young fellers. Don't look too good at all." He stood and scratched his red hair. "Injuns and white men. Renegades, most likely." His brown eyes were compassionate as he turned to Rand. "Looks like maybe they got Sarah."

Rand shuddered. He felt as though his whole body had suddenly turned to ice. Renegade white men were the worst scum to walk the earth. They lived with the Sioux and used them for their own purposes.

Jacob clapped a hand on his brother's shoulder. "Don't give up hope yet, Rand. We'll find her. White men move slower than Indians. We have a better chance of catching them now."

Rand nodded, but he knew Sarah was lost to him. He felt almost crazy with worry and grief as Rooster found the trail, and the detachment followed it up into the Laramie Mountains. The landscape grew more barren as loose rock over a bed of sand made travel more and more treacherous. As they rode, Rand told Rooster and Jacob about his ordeal and what Ben had said.

Jacob ducked under a low-hanging tree. "What if this is part of Ben's plan? Maybe he hired renegades to grab her."

Rand shook his head. "Even Ben wouldn't stoop to working with men like that."

By the time it was too dark to follow the trail any longer, they were near the peak of the mountain. The night air was already cold, and a crisp tang to the air mingled with the scent of sage and the smoke from the fire as Rand unloaded his supplies and prepared to bed down near Jacob and Isaac.

Rooster took his rifle out of its scabbard on his saddle. "I'll take the first watch." He walked over to a large boulder.

Rand lay on the hard ground and stared up at the sky, vaguely aware of the crackling fire to his right as he gazed at the bright panorama of stars. The fire pushed back the blackness of the night, but nothing could push away the blackness in his soul.

The plaintive howl of a pack of coyotes somewhere in the valley below him somehow added to his anguish. He prayed fervently for Sarah's safety, but he was so consumed with worry, he couldn't keep his thoughts together. The fire died to embers before he finally slept.

FIVE

When Sarah awoke she found herself on a pallet on a hard, dirt-packed floor. She sat up slowly and looked around the tiny one-room cabin. A rank odor rose from the grimy blanket over her, and she pushed it off with a shudder of disgust as she rose to get a better view of her surroundings.

Her head throbbed and the room spun as she took a step toward the small, oilskin-covered windows. She paused until her head cleared, then moved gingerly toward the door. She raised the latch and tugged at the door, but it refused to budge no matter how hard she pulled. She leaned her throbbing head against it and tried to think.

Those savages would be back any minute. What was she going to do? She could still see the painted face of the Indian who grabbed her. But why wasn't she at an Indian camp? And whose old cabin was this anyway?

But there were no answers to her questions, so she pushed away the fears and looked around for another avenue of escape. Her body ached in a hundred places from her contact with the thornbush, and she limped as she picked through the debris on the dirt floor.

She found a small stool among the litter of papers, old tin cans, and rags and dragged it under the window. Standing on the stool, she pulled the torn oilcloth away from the window and tried to pull herself through.

But the tiny opening was much too small for even Sarah's slim shoulders, and the stool collapsed under her weight, one leg rolling useless across the floor, as she fell to the ground. She was hungry and thirsty and scared. Judging by the light, it was close to noon, so she must have been unconscious nearly twenty-four hours. No wonder her mouth was like cotton.

She sat there until the sun no longer shone through

the east window, feeling more and more abandoned. What if she was left here to die with no food or water? Panic overwhelmed her, and she ran to the door and pounded on it. She backed away when she heard horses approaching. The click of a lock being pulled back on the door.

Trembling, she faced the door, so frightened she felt faint. If only she could see who was on the other side. Had the savages come back, or was she about to be rescued? She didn't dare hope.

The sudden flood of sunlight into the dark cabin blinded her momentarily, then she blinked in surprise as she recognized the two figures framed in the doorway.

"Be-Ben?" she croaked through her parched throat. "Thank the Lord you're here."

Although she would rather anyone else rescue her, Ben was a welcome surprise from the savages she'd expected. She had opened her mouth to thank him when she noticed how unsurprised he seemed to see her.

"Been awake long? I wanted to give you time to appreciate my appearance."

"You knew . . . I was here?" Her chest thumped hard, and she took a step back.

"Of course." He kicked some refuse away from

the door. "Shut the door, Labe." He reached out and touched a lock of her hair, and she flinched away. His lips tightened as he dropped his hand. "The Indians were eager for the guns I offered for the 'soldier girl with hair like the sun.' But I must give credit where credit's due. Jessica came up with the idea."

Sarah felt the blood drain from her face. Ben and Jessica had arranged for her kidnapping? But why? Her lips quivered as she forced back tears of weakness. She didn't want to give him the satisfaction of seeing her cry.

"Aren't you interested in why you're here?" The cruel light in Ben's eyes grew as she took a step back. "Remember that marriage we were supposed to have? You should have been my wife by now, and I aim to put that to rights." He pulled her to him and wrapped a hand in her hair.

Pain encased her head as he tightened his grip on her. "Let go of me." She couldn't hold back a moan when he pulled even harder.

"Too bad about your beloved Rand," he sneered. "You have no one to blame for his death but yourself."

A shudder shook Sarah's frame, and she closed her eyes. "Wha–what do you mean?"

"I'm sure he's dead by now." He smirked. "Being staked out in the sun without food or water isn't a pleasant way to die, but he deserved every bit of torment."

Rand dead? She *wouldn't* believe it. "You're lying," she whispered. After all, she'd believed Ben before— and look what had happened.

"Think so? Tell her, Labe."

His brother looked away and shuffled his feet. She stared into Ben's face. How had she ever considered marrying him? The silence grew heavy as Ben stared back at her with an unsettling conviction in his eyes. He'd fooled her before, though. Labe's nervous shuffle broke the silence.

Sarah turned her eyes toward him. "Please. Please, Labe. Help me."

Labe's eyes darted from his brother's set face to Sarah's. "Come on, Ben. Let's take her back. She won't say nothin', will you, Sarah?"

"No. No, of course not." She wet her dry lips with the tip of her tongue. "Just take me back to the fort, and I'll say you rescued me from the Indians. You'll be heroes."

Ben's lip curled. "You must take me for a fool!" He let go of Sarah's hair and shoved her off her feet, then spun toward Labe. "Get out!" He pushed his brother out of the door, then shut and locked it.

While Ben's back was turned, her hand groped along the dirty floor. Her seeking fingers closed around the broken stool leg. Ben turned back toward her and leaned down with a smile. She twisted around and with one last desperate effort, she smashed the stool leg against his head. He slumped against her without a sound.

She scrambled to her feet, rushed to the door, and pulled it open. She blinked as she surveyed her surroundings. The tiny cabin was in a small clearing enclosed by heavy forest. A meadow filled with wildflowers was in front of the door, and a narrow, barely discernible path ran through the middle of the meadow. She caught a glimpse of Labe's head over near a stand of aspen with his back to the cabin.

Watching to make sure Labe didn't see her, she stumbled along the path, casting furtive glances behind her to make sure neither Labe nor Ben was following her. The path narrowed further, then disappeared at the bank of a small stream. Sarah sank to her knees and drank.

Birds twittered from the budding branches above

her head, but that was the only sound as she followed the stream into the forest. The stream soon joined a larger river, and Sarah rushed along the bank. How long would it be before Ben regained consciousness? He would pursue her. She had to get as far away as she could.

Labe had fallen asleep leaning against an aspen tree, but he woke with a jump when Ben staggered out of the cabin.

"Where is she?" Ben looked around wildly.

"Who?" Labe peered past Ben into the dark cabin as if trying to see Sarah.

"Who do you think?" Ben held his aching head and tried to think. "Why didn't you stop her?"

"Honest, Ben, I didn't see nothin'." He backed away from his brother and stared slack jawed as Ben stumbled toward the horses. "Where you going? I thought we was going to hole up here for a few days."

"Plans have changed." Ben tightened the cinch on his mare's belly. "Thanks to you, I've got to track Miss Sarah down."

"Can't we just leave her be?"

Ben wiped away a bit of blood from his face. "She's not getting off after what she did to me." He swung into the saddle and waited impatiently while Labe followed suit. Ben's face burned. No one got in Ben Croftner's way without paying for it.

The sun told her it was midafternoon, and Sarah stopped beside the river. Her head was light from lack of food, and she had to rest for a moment. She sank down on a large rock and looked around, trying to think. She had to find something to eat or she'd never make it.

Wearily, she forced herself to her feet again and searched the bushes, grateful for the forest lore Rand had taught her when they were growing up. After several minutes, she found some berries she knew were edible, and she crammed handfuls into her mouth, grimacing at their bitter taste. Using her fingernails, she dug the roots of another edible plant out of the ground. She washed the soil off in the river and then crunched them down.

A little clearer-headed, she stared along the river-bank again. She would make it. She strode off with new determination.

But by the next morning, she was no longer so certain. She itched from what seemed like a thousand mosquito bites. The insects had swarmed around her all night, a living haze of biting misery. So weak now from hunger and fatigue, she could barely stagger with one foot in front of the other. She'd startled awake with every sound all night. Coyotes had howled, their voices closer than she had ever heard them, and once a large animal had snuffled right next to her, causing her to freeze, too terrified to move for several long minutes.

Now, as the sun tipped to the west, her steps slowed. She rounded a curve in the river, forcing herself forward, and then stood still.

She was face-to-face with a band of ten or so Sioux warriors. Their faces were painted and one young man had a livid scar across his cheek. The blood drained from her face, and then darkness claimed her.

SIX

Rand rode silently through the woods, hardly looking at the other men for fear he'd see the fear he felt in their eyes. Jacob reined his horse in suddenly and dismounted. He bent over and picked something off the ground.

"What is it?" Rand's voice was hoarse. He held out his hand and Jacob dropped a brooch into it.

They'd both seen it many times. The delicate filigree rose customarily adorned the bodice of Sarah's dress. Rand had given it to her for her sixteenth birthday before he left for the war. Hard to believe it had been over three years.

He stared at the dainty pin, and his face turned hard as he fought to control the pain that surged through him. "At least we know we're on the right trail. Everyone always said Rooster could follow a wood tick on solid rock." Rand picked up the reins, gripped by a renewed sense of urgency. "Let's get going."

Rooster led the way, his keen eyes following the fresh trail. They splashed across the stream and picked their way up a steep hill. He glanced around at the silent men as they paused at the top. "Reckon we all fell a little bit in love with that gal." His voice was hoarse.

"Don't say it like she's gone!" Isaac's knuckles were white where they gripped the reins. "We can't be more than a few hours behind her." He urged his horse forward and took the lead through a line of trees.

Rand and Jacob, following close behind, reined in at the sound of a startled snort. Two bear cubs bleated and rolled toward their mother. Mama bear swung around from her perusal of a fallen tree trunk, ready to face the threat to her offspring.

Rand's eyes met the grizzly's. She roared angrily

as she rose to her hind feet, a good seven feet tall. Her mouth wide with another roar, she dropped to all fours and charged toward them.

Jacob was closest, and his horse shied. He fell to the ground. The bear loomed over him and opened her giant mouth. He grabbed for his gun, but it lay three feet away where it had fallen from his holster when he was catapulted from the saddle. He scrabbled backward, away from the grizzly.

"Lie still, boy!" Rooster aimed his Winchester at the bear's head, just as Rand frantically aimed his own gun.

The rifles barked, but not before the grizzly swiped at Jacob's leg with her claws. She swung her head in dull surprise, then crashed to the ground beside Jacob.

Blood was already pouring from Jacob's leg, soaking his torn pants. "Quick, hand me the canteen!" Rand fell to his knees beside his brother.

Rooster handed him the canteen. "Clean it good, boy, or it'll fester for sure. No telling where that bear's claws have been."

Rand ripped the fabric away from the wound and splashed it with water again and again. Jacob's flesh was flayed so badly that the bone gleamed through the shredded skin. Rand tried to keep the dismay from his face as he bound the wound with a clean handkerchief.

Jacob's face was pale and sweat sheened his forehead as he gritted his teeth against the pain. "Sorry, Rand." His face contracted frustration. "We were so close."

Rand patted his brother's leg. "You're going to be all right." He prayed the words were true. But he couldn't abandon Sarah. Somehow he had to arrange to get Jacob back to the fort while he pressed on to find her.

Isaac crouched beside him and gave Jacob a sip of water. "How bad is it?"

Rand turned his head away so Jacob couldn't hear. "Bad. It's deep in his thigh muscle—to the bone. He'll be in even more pain when the shock wears off. We need to find someplace for him to hole up." He paused bleakly. "He won't be riding for a while."

Isaac nodded. "I hunted this area last year. If I remember right, there's a small cabin just beyond the woods to our north. Let's make for there. It's almost dark anyway."

Rand fought to keep despair from settling in as they made a rough travois to carry Jacob. This delay could be deadly for Sarah.

Isaac led the way through the trees. Rand spared a thought for the motherless bear cubs, but there was nothing they could do for them. He found himself smiling, thinking that if Sarah were there, she would probably have insisted they catch the cubs and bring them home to raise. His smile faded to a frown of pain as he was washed anew with fear for Sarah.

The light was murky by the time they stepped out of the forest and into a small meadow clearing. The cabin squatted against the sloping north side, and they hurried toward its meager haven.

The open door creaked in the gentle breeze as they swung off their horses. "Me and the men will take care of the horses," Rooster said. "Git that boy inside. Better clean the wound again too."

Rand and Isaac carefully lifted Jacob off the travois and carried him into the dark cabin. They laid him on a moldy mattress in the corner.

"Light a lantern, Isaac." Rand eased his brother's boots off and untied the handkerchief on Jacob's leg.

Isaac lit the lantern, and the dim glow pushed the shadows back. The wound had reopened from the jostling on the travois, and Jacob lay unconscious.

One of the other men came in with a small flask in

his hand. "Rooster says he brought it along for medicinal purposes."

Rand uncapped the flask and poured a generous amount of alcohol into Jacob's gaping wound. He thrashed and cried out, then lapsed back into unconsciousness as Rand rebound the wound.

"I reckon that's all we can do," he said to Isaac.

"Except pray."

Rand looked at Isaac, then back at his brother. He nodded and knelt on the floor, Isaac beside him as they each asked God for his help. After a few minutes, Isaac got to his feet, but Rand stayed where he was. At last he stood, and a new peace filled his heart. He felt his first real sense of hope that they might find Sarah alive and well.

They made up their beds on the dirt floor. Rand checked on Jacob several times throughout the night as his brother thrashed restlessly. Finally at dawn, he touched Jacob's forehead and found it cool. He breathed a sigh as he pulled on his boots and woke the others.

The first rays of sunrise pushed through bare branches as Rand sat eating a cold breakfast of hardtack and dried meat under a tree. They had to find her today.

Rooster burst into the clearing. "She was here! Our little gal was here!"

Rand jumped up and gripped Rooster's arm. "What are you talking about?"

"Our Sarah was here. Look!" Rooster held out a scrap of familiar green-and-yellow calico.

Rand fingered the soft cloth. "Where did you find it?" He pressed it against his lips and inhaled, but there was no lingering fragrance other than of mud.

"Down by the stream. And I found her trail—she's alone." Rooster almost danced in jubilation.

Rand stared at the scrap of fabric, almost giddy with relief. She'd gotten away from whoever had held her captive. "Let's check Jacob."

When he stepped into the cabin, he found Jacob sitting up, sipping a thin gruel made of water and hardtack. He gave them a wan smile. "Sorry, Rand. Guess I won't be in any shape to travel for a few days."

Rand nodded. "I'm just thankful you're alive." He grinned, eager to wipe the look of guilt off Jacob's face. "I have to wonder, though, if you didn't get in that bear's way just so you'd have a good story to tell back at Bedlam."

He waited until Jacob smiled weakly, and then Rand turned to the group of privates who were crouching against the wall eating their hardtack. "I want you soldiers to stay with Jacob until he can travel, then get him back to the fort. Isaac and Rooster will come with me to find Sarah." He cocked an eyebrow at his two friends. "Okay with you?"

"Let's get going." Isaac's eyes were hooded.

Rand eyed him. He hadn't even stopped to think how this was affecting Isaac. Their affection for the same woman wasn't something either of them would be comfortable talking about either.

Rooster nodded. "I'll saddle up the horses."

Fifteen minutes later, Rand was almost jubilant as they followed Sarah's clear trail.

"That gal will never make an Injun," Rooster muttered. "She leaves a path even a greenhorn could follow."

Near noon, they rounded a bend in the river they were following and Rooster stopped short. He whistled in dismay. Sarah's clear tracks were obliterated by unshod pony tracks and moccasin prints. "Looks like the Injuns caught her."

Rand stood staring at the telltale marks, his heart pounding. So close to finding her and now this. He swallowed hard as he fought to hold on to his new faith and hope. "Can you tell what kind of Indians?"

"Hard to say, but I'd guess Sioux."

They followed the trail for the rest of the afternoon. Rand struggled to pray, but despair kept rearing its head.

One of the Sioux warriors gave Sarah jerky and fresh water before jabbering and pulling her to her feet. In spite of her terror, she was grateful for the food. She'd never been so hungry in her life. The jerky was tough, but she didn't know when anything had tasted so good.

She turned and looked back at the way they'd come. If Rand lived, he would find her. She was sure of it.

The young warrior with the scar on his face pulled her up behind him on his pony, and she wrinkled her nose at the stench of sweat and bear grease. The Sioux band picked its way along a faint trail through the forest. Sarah would never have recognized it was a trail, but once they had followed it for a while, she was able to see the slight impression from other Indian ponies. Twilight was sending out long, golden shadows by the time they turned the crest of a hill. Campfires and teepee shapes became visible below them in the valley beside a stream.

Children jabbered and women stared at her with hostile eyes as the warriors paraded through the camp, raising their bows and spears in triumphant shrieks. Sarah fought unconsciousness as she tried not to droop wearily against the young warrior's back. Her vision blurred and doubled as he stopped beside a teepee and slid to the ground.

He pulled her down, and she fought his grip on her arms. "Let go of me."

He grunted, then thrust her inside the teepee and closed the flap, encasing her in darkness. She was too weary to do more than stumble to a soft pile of furs and sink into instant sleep.

When Sarah awoke she was in a dark, cool place. Strange chanting filled her head, and she heard the rumbles of unfamiliar voices. But the words were all jumbled together, and nothing made any sense. She tried to rise and was surprised to find she could move her hands and feet. She had thought the Indians would tie her up so she couldn't escape in the night. The sounds outside were distant and not threatening, so she snuggled back down in the furs and fell asleep again.

The next time she awoke, she was not alone. A beautiful Indian girl knelt beside her and offered her a bowl of stew that smelled wonderful. She took it and ate eagerly. It was flavored with unfamiliar herbs, but the meat and vegetables were tasty. The young woman smiled, then quickly stepped outside and closed the flap on the teepee behind her.

Sarah's shoulder protested as she got to her feet. Swaying weakly, she started toward the flap, then staggered and sank back to the ground. She was just too tired to push herself any longer. She returned to the bearskin rug and stared at the opening to the teepee. What if Rand was really dead like Ben said? She pushed the thought away. He couldn't be dead. And he would find her.

She looked around curiously. She'd always wondered

what a teepee looked like inside, but she'd never been in one. Not even Morning Song's.

The teepee was large, at least ten feet in diameter. In the center was a tripod arrangement that supported a pot over what were now cold ashes, although a pile of buffalo chips lay heaped to the side. Spears and knives hung from the lodge poles, and buffalo robes were piled to one side. Pelts of various animals—dove, wolverine, raccoon, and antelope—were in various stages of tanning on a rack of some kind.

She dragged her gaze away from the lodge furnishings as the flap opened and the Indian warrior came in. A fierce scowl creased his young face, and Sarah's heart pounded in trepidation. It was the youth with the terrible scar on his cheek she'd seen before.

"He–hello," she stammered. Then she smiled as she remembered the Sioux greeting Isaac had taught her. *"Wash ta cola."*

He merely grunted, his black eyes roaming over Sarah's tangled hair. He reached out and touched a bright red-gold lock.

She forced herself not to flinch. "Sarah." She gestured at herself. "My name is Sarah."

The warrior nodded, a smile winking across his face so quickly Sarah thought she'd imagined it.

The flap lifted again as the young Sioux maiden entered. She reminded Sarah of a young antelope, all long limbs yet curiously graceful. Sarah's heart clenched as she thought of Morning Song.

"You awake," she said, her dark eyes liquid with a hidden smile.

"You speak English." Sarah smiled in relief.

"Little. Little English. Live at mission one year." The girl squatted and offered her another bowl of stew. "You eat."

Sarah wasn't really hungry any longer, but since she intended to escape at the first opportunity, she needed to build up her strength as quickly as possible.

The boy grunted again and said something to the girl. "Little Wolverine say you belong to blue coat with eyes like eagle. Soldier not kill Little Wolverine in battle. Why?"

Sarah searched her memory, but she couldn't remember Rand mentioning an incident like he described. "I don't know," she admitted reluctantly.

The girl translated to the young man and he fired a volley of words back at her. "He say blue coat with eagle eyes spare Little Wolverine. Little Wolverine save you." She pretended to weigh her hands until they were on an equal level.

"Yes. Even. Thank you." Sarah looked into the dark eyes beside her and thanked God for sending such an unlikely rescuer. They weren't going to hurt her.

SEVEN

Sarah's strength grew daily on the good food White Dove brought. She gave Sarah a beautifully beaded Indian dress to replace her torn dress and braided her hair.

Sarah and the young maiden grew to be friends— she felt an almost uncanny sense of friendship and identification with her, as if she'd known her all her life—and by the third day Sarah felt at home in the busy Sioux camp. The children were curious about her and soon lost their shyness when she appeared.

White Dove was happy to translate their innumerable questions.

But Sarah grew more anxious daily. Where was Rand? Was there any truth to what Ben told her? Could Rand really be dead—or did he think she was dead? And Joel would be frantic. What would become of her little brother if Sarah never returned? She couldn't bear to think of him with Wade. Maybe Amelia and Jacob would raise him.

"Why you so sad?" White Dove asked as they fished in the stream just after dawn on the fourth day.

Sarah clambered out of the water and sat on a large rock, White Dove following close behind her. "I miss my friends and my little brother. You know the word *brother*?"

White Dove nodded. "I have small brother." She held out her hand to her waist.

"And I worry about the bad man who tried to hurt me. He may be looking for me still."

White Dove nodded slowly, her dark eyes compassionate. "Little Wolverine take you back soon. Then debt to blue coat is paid. And Little Wolverine say Sarah cry no more. He know man who hurt Sarah. He make sure he not hurt Sarah again." She reached over and touched Sarah's arm shyly. "White Dove miss Sarah."

"I'll miss you too," she said hoarsely. "Thank Little Wolverine for me. You are both good friends."

Just a few days with the Sioux had shown her how alike they all were. Little Wolverine and the other Indians had no idea how many settlers were clamoring to take away the Indian hunting grounds. And Rand might actually have to fight Little Wolverine some day. She couldn't stand the thought of the bright young warrior lying dead on a field of battle.

She picked up her string of fish and followed White Dove back to camp. Why was life never simple?

Rand and his companions followed the trail as it led through rocky hills and sagebrush-choked gullies. When they ran low on rations, Rand and Isaac brought down an antelope and cut it into strips for jerky, smoking it overnight over a low fire. Rand alternated between worry for Sarah and concern for Jacob back at the cabin.

Four days from the fort, they awoke to a leaden

sky with a stiff, moisture-laden breeze whipping across the stark landscape. If it rained, the trail would be washed away. And they were so close. They hurriedly saddled up and rode out.

But their haste was useless. The storm struck with its usual force in the mountains. Hail rained down on them, and they were forced to take shelter under an overhang in the gully. Thunder boomed around them as torrents of rain fell and lightning crackled overhead.

"We've got to git to high ground!" Rooster shouted above the crashing thunder. "This here's a real gully washer. There's liable to be a flash flood any time."

Staying as close to the rock wall as possible, they led their horses up the rocky hill. Halfway up the side of the slope, Rand looked down. A mountain of water swept away the tangle of sagebrush and aspen where they'd been only minutes before.

"This here's prob'ly high enough." Rooster paused under an overhang.

They crouched there, hugging the cold side of the rocky wall. The horses shifted restlessly, but the men managed to hang on to the reins. Finally the downpour was over. Steamy mist shimmered in the heat as the sun broke through the clouds, and they emerged from their sanctuary.

Rand gaped at the changed landscape. The flash flood had carved new gullies and filled in old low spots as the raging water carried away everything in its path. He stood surveying the damage as dismay swept over him. The trail to Sarah would never have survived such rain.

"Don't take on so, boy. We ain't done by a long shot."

"What do you mean, Rooster? How will we ever find her now?"

"I've scouted these parts before. Over yonder peak is one of the Injuns' favorite camping grounds. We'll just mosey on over there, and maybe we'll find our little gal."

Galvanized, Rand leaped astride his horse as Rooster led the way and Isaac brought up the rear. By nightfall they were in a line of trees overlooking an Indian campground. The teepees glowed with color from the sunset. They caught glimpses of dimly illuminated figures moving around the campfires.

"Now what?" Rand asked.

"Now we stay put till they're sleepin'." The old Indian fighter took off his hat and smoothed his red hair. "Then we sneak in and look around for our Miss Sarah."

They tied their horses to a tree and hunkered down to wait. Rand kept watch while the other two tried to catch a little sleep. He was just about to wake Isaac for his turn at watch when he noticed a movement just below their lookout. He cocked his rifle and the other two were awake in an instant.

"What is it?" Isaac whispered.

"Don't know. Thought I saw something." Rand searched the spot again, but he froze when he heard a sound on the slope above them. He swiveled his head and faced a row of fiercely painted Indians holding spears, all pointed at him and his friends.

They were obviously outnumbered, so when one of the Indians motioned for them to drop their guns, they obeyed. The Sioux bound their hands with brutal efficiency, then marched them down the slope to the camp. They thrust them roughly into a large teepee and fastened the flap firmly behind them.

Rand could see the outline of a guard through the buckskin. Some rescuers they were. Now they were all in the same uncomfortable spot with Sarah, if she was even here.

Rand squatted on a buffalo robe. "Why didn't they kill us outright?"

"They're probably saving us for some special ceremony," Isaac said, sitting down on a buffalo robe. "We'd best get some sleep. They'll be on their guard tonight, but maybe tomorrow we can find a way to escape."

Rand sat up just before dawn, too keyed up to lay down any longer. He listened to the sounds of the camp beginning to stir around him. He understood none of the guttural language outside as women lit fires and called to one another.

Diffused light gradually lifted the darkness inside their teepee as the bustle outside increased. Finally the flap lifted, and a young man stepped through, followed by an Indian girl. Rand immediately recognized him as the warrior he had spared in the battle the week before. And he was the one whose face he'd seen in his delirium.

Rooster recognized the boy too. "I told you you'd be sorry."

But Rand felt no fear as he looked into the youth's calm, dark eyes.

The girl stepped forward and smiled at him. "Do

not fear. Little Wolverine your friend. But he ask, 'Why you not shoot him?'"

Rand hesitated. His reasons would probably sound silly, but there was no help for it. "Little Wolverine reminded me of my younger brother. You know the word *brother*?"

The girl nodded. "One who shares mother and father?"

Rand nodded. "I have a younger brother about the same age as Little Wolverine. I saw that same brave spirit in Little Wolverine."

The girl smiled as she translated. The youth's black eyes never left Rand's face as she explained. Then he nodded and barked an order to the girl. She gave Rand a slight smile, then slipped out of the teepee. Moments later Sarah stepped through the flap behind the Indian girl.

"Sarah!"

Her green eyes widened and she gasped as Rand started toward her. "Rand?" She ran into his open arms.

Sarah burrowed her face in the rough fabric of Rand's shirt. His strong arms encased her, and she never wanted to leave this embrace she'd thought she'd never feel again. "How did you find me?"

"Rooster." He touched the bruise on her cheek, then frowned when she flinched. "Who did this to you? And how'd you get away from the renegades who had you?"

Just past him, she saw Isaac staring at the two of them. What was he thinking? She pushed away from Rand. "I–I came to a cabin." He wouldn't understand. Last time Ben had tried to force her to marry him, Rand jumped to the wrong conclusion. "Later," she whispered. She turned to the two Sioux standing silent behind her. "I would have died if it weren't for my friends. I'd like you to meet Little Wolverine and White Dove."

Rand held out his hand to the two Sioux. "I don't know what to say—how to thank you."

The girl smiled. "Sarah is friend. We miss her. You leave in morning for soldier fort but first we have feast."

Rooster and Isaac crowded close and hugged Sarah. Isaac's hug was brief, and he quickly stepped back. She hated to see the hurt in his eyes. "Thanks for saving me."

"I'm glad you're all right." He moved to the side of the teepee and folded muscular arms over his chest.

Rooster grabbed her in a bear hug. "No how were we going home without you."

She hugged him back, unashamed of the tears of joy that trickled down her cheeks. "Thank you, Rooster. They couldn't have found me without you."

She wanted to get Rand alone, to find out what Ben had tried to do to him. And how did she tell him about Jessica's role in her capture? Was it even true?

White Dove motioned to Rand. "Your wound. I will heal."

He sat down and let her smear an ointment on his wound. The stench made Sarah wrinkle her nose, but Rand endured the young woman's ministrations.

Sarah glanced at Isaac, who continued to stare at her as if he was trying to puzzle out something. This ordeal had shown her how deep her feelings for Rand still ran. How could she marry someone else when she knew she'd never get over Rand?

She joined Isaac by the teepee opening. "You have questions. I can see them in your eyes."

"I think the answers are clear. I'd hoped you'd find me a suitable substitute for Rand, but I can see that is never going to happen."

She looked down at the dirt floor. "I don't think so either. I like you, Isaac, so much. I'm sorry."

"Don't be. Better to find out now. I think he knows his own heart now too."

Her pulse throbbed in her neck, but an ache settled over her heart. "I wish that were true, but even if he realized he still loves me, he's a man of honor. He won't go back on his word to Jessica."

Reeking of something that smelled like rotting flesh, Rand joined them. "Sounds like a lot of commotion outside."

Sarah heard it then, the noise of horses and voices. She motioned to White Dove and Little Wolverine. "What's going on?"

The two Sioux walked nearer. White Dove glanced at Sarah, then back to Rand. "We go to make war with Red Cloud at Powder River."

Rand shook his head and looked hard at the young warrior. "Don't go, Little Wolverine. I don't want anything to happen to you. Tell him not to go," he appealed to White Dove.

The boy drew himself up straight and taut as White Dove translated. "He say, 'Should Little Wolverine stay in camp like dog and let others fight for his family? Soon people have no hunting grounds. Whites take all. Red Cloud say Indians must fight or be forced to farm.'"

The boy spat in the dust. "He say, 'Lakota not dirt diggers.'" Little Wolverine's face softened as he spoke again and White Dove continued to translate. "But he say, 'Rand and Little Wolverine brothers. They not fight.'"

"No, my brother." Rand laid a hand on Little Wolverine's shoulder. "We'll not fight. And someday I hope we meet again."

The boy clasped his hand over Rand's large, square hand as though he understood his words before White Dove translated them. His dark eyes were warm with friendship.

Sarah's heart squeezed at the thought of the hardships coming to her new friends. There was nothing she could do either. Nothing any of them could do. The fight for western lands would not be over anytime soon.

EIGHT

Amelia watched the hills surrounding the fort every day, anxious for word of Sarah. The main detachment had returned, hauling Jacob home two days ago, but no one had heard a word from the three who pushed on after Sarah. Her husband paced their small quarters as he waited for word of his brother. When she'd first seen his wound, she'd shuddered, but Jacob was recovering much better than she'd feared.

After breakfast on the third day of Jacob's return, Amelia sat on the porch, watching as the cavalry prepared for maneuvers. Joel sat listlessly beside her, and she put her hand on his arm. "Hang on to your hope, Joel. Maybe Jacob will have news when he gets back."

Tears hung on his lashes. "He has to find her. He has to!"

She touched his cheek. "He will."

"Boots and saddles." Captain Brown shouted the familiar command to mount, and the cavalry swung up onto their horses and rode out of the fort.

Jacob limped across the parade ground to join her and Joel. "The commander says there is still no word. They haven't shown up at Fort Caspar or the Platte River Bridge Station."

Amelia burst into tears and jumped up to bury her face against Jacob's chest. "I have a terrible feeling she's dead. And we'll never know for sure."

Jacob held her close, and she tried to take comfort from his strength. She had a dreadful feeling she'd never see any of them again.

Joel stood suddenly and pointed west. "What's that?"

Jacob turned and looked, then grew still, his gaze scanning the slope to the west of the fort. He pulled Amelia away. "Wait here."

"What is it?"

She shaded her eyes with her hand and saw four riders coming down the rocky incline toward the fort. And one of them, dressed in buckskin like an Indian maiden, had sunny red-gold hair. With a sob of relief, she picked up her skirts and ran after Jacob.

"They've got her!" a sentry to the west of the fort shouted as soldiers ran from the mess hall and barracks to greet their beloved Sarah. Amelia wasn't the only one who had just about given up hope.

Soldiers lined the road and cheered as the four travelers, tired and dusty, rode into the fort.

"Sarah!"

With a sob of joy, Sarah slipped off her mare and fell into Amelia's arms. Laughing and crying, she hugged Amelia, then Joel as soldiers cheered and whistled and slapped each other on the backs. Even the post commander was out to greet them.

Amelia looked up at Rand. "I knew you'd find her."

He grinned down at her. "Always. I'll never let her go."

Amelia caught her breath. Did he mean what she thought he meant?

Joel clung to Sarah as they walked home. *Home.* She'd never thought to see this modest house again. Rand laughed as he tried to tell their story. But the true story still had to be told.

Amelia sent Joel out with the men, then heated a kettle of water and poured it into a hip bath as Sarah peeled off the dusty, stained buckskin dress. She poured cold water into the bath and tested to make sure it wasn't too hot, then as Sarah eased in with a sigh, Amelia began to comb the tangles out of her friend's red-gold locks.

A half hour later, hair washed and clad in clean clothes, Sarah curled up on the sofa while Amelia stood over her, plaiting Sarah's hair into a long braid. "You have so many bruises. But of course the Indians are notorious for their brutality."

Her friend's sympathetic touch and voice broke the dam on Sarah's emotions, and she burst into tears. She had to tell someone—she couldn't hold it inside any longer. "It wasn't the Indians, Amelia—they helped me. It was Ben."

Amelia's fingers in Sarah's hair stilled. "Ben Croftner? He beat you?" Her voice was incredulous, and she curled her hands into fists.

Sarah nodded. In a flood, the horror of her ordeal gushed out. Amelia sat and held her as she choked out the truth.

"Did you tell Rand?" White with shock and disbelief, Amelia pushed the hair out of Sarah's face, then held her close again.

"No. But I know I have to." Sarah pulled back and laced her hands together. "I–I just couldn't face it. He'll hate me, I know it. You know how jealous he is of Ben." She shuddered. "What if he thinks I encouraged him? What if he doesn't believe me when I tell him I got away before Ben could—?"

The words hung in the air. Amelia placed her hand over Sarah's hands. "Oh, Sarah, he'll believe you. He's learned to trust again these last few months. And I'm sure he doesn't blame you anymore. It wasn't your fault."

The front door banged open, and they both turned as Rand, Joel, and Jacob strode into the room.

Rand's face brightened when he saw Sarah. "You look much better."

"Well, I'm starved. How 'bout you, honey?" Jacob pulled Amelia to her feet. "Let's go get some grub at the mess hall." They started toward the door. "Come with us, half-pint," he told Joel. "We won't be late," he called over his shoulder.

The ploy to leave them alone was too obvious to be missed, and Sarah suppressed a smile. "I'll fix you some flapjacks." Rand stared at her arm, and she pulled her shawl over the bruises there.

"I'm not hungry yet. We need to talk. I want to know what happened. You've been avoiding my questions. And I have some things to tell you too."

Sarah sat back down abruptly. She was tired of worrying about his reaction. There was only one way to find out. "I was afraid you'd blame me, but I swear to you I had no idea he would try something like that."

"Who are you talking about?"

"Ben. He hired some Laramie loafers to grab me," she blurted the words out in a rush, then hurried on as his face darkened. "When I came to, I was in a locked cabin by myself. Ben showed up—" She drew a ragged breath. "He—he said we should have been married by then. He . . ." Her words trailed away at the irate expression on his face.

"That no-good skunk. So that's what he meant." Rand leaned over and touched her arm. "He gave you those bruises? Did he—did he hurt you in any other way?"

She shook her head. "I hit him over the head with a stool leg and knocked him out cold. Then I took off and got away while he was out. Labe was there too, but he wasn't watching the cabin. What did you mean, 'that's what he meant'? When did you talk to him?"

Rand drew a couple of deep breaths, then grabbed his hat.

"Where are you going?"

"To find Jessica. I have some unfinished business to take care of." He came back and kissed her quickly. "Don't go outside the grounds. I might not be lucky enough to find you a second time. Don't look so worried. I'll tell the whole story when I get back." He gazed down into her eyes, then stroked her cheek. "I know it wasn't your fault, Green Eyes."

She watched him go with some relief. He did trust her after all. "Be careful," she called after his retreating back.

Jessica looked up as her mother ushered Rand into the parlor, then left them alone. "Darling." She rose to her feet. "I didn't know you were back." She lifted her face for a kiss, but Rand just stared at her impassively. "What is it? What's wrong?"

"Your little plan failed."

"Whatever do you mean?" Her blue eyes looked huge and innocent.

Rand could see behind her beauty now. She was like a snake, gorgeous coloring but a deadly bite. "I know all about it, Jessica. Ben told me the whole story when he tried to kill me."

Her eyes widened. "Ben who? Who tried to kill you?"

Rand could see the pulse beating quickly in her throat. She was a smooth one all right. "You and Ben schemed to kidnap Sarah to get her away from me. You knew I still loved her. Don't bother to deny it. And it almost worked. But I found her, and we pieced together what the two of you cooked up between you."

Jessica's face whitened. "How could you prefer that little milksop to me?" She put her hand to her mouth, and her eyes filled with tears. "I love you, Rand. I didn't want to lose you. Surely you can see I had to do something. I could see the hold she had over you."

"I love her. I always have." He saw her flinch but went on anyway. "I tried to deceive myself, but I can't any longer. How could you do such a thing? If people just knew the evil that hides behind that beautiful mask of yours! You can consider our engagement off, of course." He put his hat on and stalked toward the door.

"Wait, Rand!" Jessica ran after him and caught his sleeve. "I know you love me. We can work this out."

He shook her hand off. "All I feel for you is contempt." He didn't wait to see the effect of his words but slammed the door behind him.

That was over. Now to find Croftner. He stopped to see the colonel, who readily agreed to let him take six men out to look for Ben and try to bring him in.

After two days Rand had no luck in picking up Ben's trail. Reluctantly, he turned toward Fort Laramie and home. He hated to face Sarah with his failure. Neither one of them could rest until they knew the threat Ben posed was eliminated.

He paused atop a bluff, took a swig from his canteen, then led the men down the slope. "Lieutenant, over here!" One of the men waved from the top of the bluff.

Rand trotted over to where the men stood. A body lay facedown in a ravine. He rolled the man over and gasped. It was Labe. He groaned, and Rand turned to hail one of his men. "Get me my canteen." He poured a little water into Labe's mouth. "Easy, now. Not too much," he cautioned as Labe tried to sit up to suck more water down.

"Indians!" Labe moaned and thrashed around as Rand drew the canteen away.

"They're gone. You're with friends now."

"Rand?" Labe peered up at him. "I'm sorry 'bout poor little Sarah. I tried to talk Ben out of it, but he wouldn't listen to no reason."

"Where is Ben?"

Tears welled up in Labe's eyes. "Dead. Indians attacked us. Ben fought them, but he fell off his horse and hit his head. "I–I buried him over there." He pointed to a long pile of rocks.

Rand patted his shoulder. "How'd you get away?"

"They left me here." He touched his head gingerly. "They must have hit me on the head."

"You'll be all right. We just need to get you back to the fort." He helped Labe to his feet and helped him up into the saddle. It was a long way back to Fort Laramie.

The week flew by as Sarah immersed herself in activity. She tried to still the worry as she thought of Rand out looking for Ben. On Monday, Wednesday, and Friday morning she taught the Indian children. Living with the Sioux for those four days gave her a new love and tenderness for the dark-eyed youngsters who crowded into the small church. She delighted in seeing their solemn faces break into smile.

She had just gotten back from school when Joel burst into the parlor. "Rand's back!" She jumped to her feet and followed him onto the porch where she saw a familiar set of broad shoulders striding toward her across the parade ground. With a cry, she ran into his open arms.

He hugged her tightly, then led her back inside the house. Joel jabbered excitedly as he followed them. "I need to talk to your sister for a few minutes alone, half-pint. Can you find something else to do for a little while?"

"Sure. Tommy Justice, the new lieutenant's son, said he'd play baseball with me."

"Thanks." Rand turned back to Sarah. "Sit down

here with me. We have a lot to talk about." He took her hand.

Sarah sat beside him, her heart pounding at his solemn face.

"Ben's dead." He told her what Labe had told him and then the entire story of Ben's plot.

Sarah was surprised at her own reaction. She felt unexplainable sadness over Ben's wasted life, although he had received his just reward. "I read a verse this morning. It said, 'And he shall bring upon them their own iniquity, and shall cut them off in their own wickedness; yea, the Lord our God shall cut them off.'"

Rand nodded. "But Jessica was in on it too. And God hasn't cut her off."

She squeezed his hand as the words sank in. "That was the plan I heard them talking about."

He nodded again. "The whole thing was her idea." He raked a hand through his dark hair. "Not that Ben wouldn't have come up with something himself."

"Why would she do such a thing?"

"To get you away from me." He stared into her face. "She sensed I still had feelings for you." He shook his head. "I had no idea she was capable of such an act of vengeance."

Her heart surged at his admission in spite of her shock. He did still love her. "That's why she left Fort Laramie in such a hurry." She saw his questioning look. "She left the day after you did. She's going to Boston with her mother."

"I see." He took a deep breath. "I wanted to tell you at the Sioux encampment, but I felt it was only right that I break things off with Jessica first. I've been a fool, Sarah. I never stopped loving you. I've never loved anyone but you."

She laid a hand on his cheek. "There's nothing to forgive. I've always loved you."

He caught her hand and brought her palm to his lips. "Will you marry me?"

"When?" Her stomach was playing mumblety-peg as he kissed her palm lingeringly.

"Today wouldn't be too soon." He put an arm around her and pulled her onto his lap. "I love you so much, Green Eyes. Even when I told myself I hated you, deep down I knew better." He traced a finger along the curve of her smooth cheek, then bent his head.

As his lips found hers, tears slipped out of Sarah's eyes. She put her arms around his neck as the kiss became more urgent. When he pulled away, she slid her fingers through the rough thatch of his hair.

"Let's not wait too long to marry," he whispered. "I want you all to myself."

"Me too," she said, blushing. "But what about Joel?"

"He'll live with us, of course. I love him like a brother. But I think Jacob will keep him for a week or so while we settle into married life."

She'd known he loved Joel, but it soothed her to hear him say the words. She nestled her face against his shirt.

COLLEEN LOVES TO HEAR FROM HER READERS!

Be sure to sign up for Colleen's newsletter for insider information on deals and appearances.

Visit her website at www.colleencoble.com
Twitter: @colleencoble
Facebook: colleencoblebooks

ABOUT THE AUTHOR

Photo by Clik Chick Photography

RITA finalist Colleen Coble is the author of several bestselling romantic suspense novels, including *Tidewater Inn*, and the Mercy Falls, Lonestar, and Rock Harbor series.